# LV48

## The Cassie Tam Files, Book Three

*Matt Doyle*

A NineStar Press Publication

Published by NineStar Press
P.O. Box 91792,
Albuquerque, New Mexico, 87199 USA.
www.ninestarpress.com

LV48



Printed in the USA
First Edition
December, 2018

Print ISBN: 978-1-949909-64-7

Also available in eBook, ISBN: 978-1-949909-62-3

Warning: This book contains scenes of violence.

# Chapter One

*"NEI HOU GAAU siu."*

When Lori smiles like that, her eyes take on a slight twinkle, making their pale blue tone feel warm and welcoming. That being the case, it takes me a moment to realise I didn't understand a word she just said. Am I so drunk already? "Uh, sorry. What?"

Lori giggles and repeats, *"Nei hou gaau siu."* When I stare blankly, she frowns and asks, "Is my pronunciation off? I was sure that was right."

"What were you trying to say?"

"I was trying to tell you that you're funny in Cantonese."

And at that, the laughter spills out of me, uncontrolled to the point I have to bury my face in the table to muffle the sound. If we'd been in our usual haunt, Northern Main Street's late-night café-cum-alternative hangout Tourniquet, I'd have let loose uninhibited. The people there look like an odd bunch when you're viewing things from the outside, but if you spend enough time there, you soon realise they're all really nice people with tastes and hobbies that fall outside the mainstream. Seeing as we've opted for Cartwright's on Dunstone Avenue, though, I'm trying to hold back. Honestly, I am. I'm just not doing a good job of it.

The staff in Cartwright's are lovely, but the clientele is a little less raucous than those at Tourniquet, and so I'm already drawing some confused looks by the time I wipe the tears from my eyes. "I'm sorry," I say, "I'm sorry."

"I've never been much good at languages. Oh God," Lori sighs and shoots me a now far more nervous smile. "Put me out of my misery. What did I say?"

I shrug. "You probably told me I was funny in Cantonese."

Lori tilts her head and says, "Okay, now I'm confused."

"I don't speak Cantonese."

"Yes, you do."

"I really don't."

"You *really* do. I mean, you can't seriously be telling me you've been using *diu* in the Taiwanese sense?"

"No, no...," I reply, waving my hands in frantic motions. "Wait. What does it mean in Taiwan?"

"It was old slang for cool."

"Oh, right. No, I'm definitely using it the way you think."

"So you *do* speak Cantonese then."

"No, I *swear* in Cantonese. I couldn't hold a conversation in it. My dad had a thing about me swearing. He hated it, even when I was an adult. It was the one thing that always made him roll his eyes at Mom. Anyway, he spoke Mandarin, English, and a little French, so my options for big kid words were kinda limited. I went to school with a guy named Tom Huang; he spoke Cantonese, so I got him to teach me the *cool* words. Dad probably got the gist of what I was saying, but I think he appreciated the ingenuity of it."

And now, Lori laughs and buries her face in her hands. She shakes her head and says, "I am such an idiot."

"Nah, it's not like I've ever spoken Mandarin around you, so how would you know? Honestly, I know enough Mandarin to get by, but we always spoke English at home, so I just picked that up easier. Let's see, though...you would have meant *nǐ hěn gǎoxiào*. Or if you wanted to be really over the top with it, *nǐ jiǎng shénme dōu néng bǎ wǒ lè huài le*. That's 'everything you say cracks me up.'"

Lori shakes her head. "I think I'll stick to English."

"I am sorry for laughing," I say, taking her hand. "It was really sweet of you to try learning something in another language for me. Why *that* phrase, though?"

Lori lets out a short, gentle laugh, and replies, "Every time we're together, you either do or say something to make me laugh, so I figured it was something I could guarantee I'd get to use."

"I'll get us another drink," I blurt, and whip myself to my feet and away towards the counter. It was just a compliment, but still... *Did I move quick enough to stop her seeing how red my cheeks are?*

"*Nǐ hěn gǎoxiào*," Lori giggles in broken Mandarin.

*I guess I was too slow. Diu.*


"YOU'RE SURE YOU don't want me to give you a lift back?" Lori asks.

I shake my head. "We both have early starts tomorrow, and it'll take you all the way back to the other end of the city. Besides, it's a nice evening."

Lori looks up at the clear sky and nods. "It's still pretty early by our standards too, so I guess it's not like there are going to be too many muggers out."

"Come on." I act mock taken aback. "You can't seriously think I wouldn't be able to handle a couple of petty thieves?"

"Oh, I know you can. I just thought if anyone was stupid enough to attack you, you'd probably get hauled up for assault."

"Cheeky," I retort, giving Lori a playful punch in the arm.

She smiles in response and draws me into a deep kiss, running her fingers smoothly through my hair and tracing a line down the back of my neck. When I shiver and a low moan leaves my lips, she pulls back and fixes me with a playful, I-love-having-that-effect-on-you grin. Ever the tease, she backs up to her car, keeping her eyes on mine, unlocks the door with the fingerprint scanner and slides effortlessly into the driver's seat. It's so well practised, part of me has always wondered if she's used the same moves on other people before. I tried following that train of thought once and came to two conclusions. The first was the concept probably wasn't new, and she knows full well what she's doing, but with others, different spots probably set them off.

The second thing I realised was that I don't really care. Whether she's treated others the same or not doesn't matter. What matters is it's *me* she's putting the effort in with now. No matter who it was for in the past, right now it's for me, and just me. Part of me really wants to tell her all that, because I want her to know how much I appreciate that she pays attention to what I like. *But you won't tell her*, I remind myself. *Because* you're *making the effort not to overanalyse things and* pretending *you don't is the best you've got right now.*

Lori slows the car as she passes me and leans out the window to say, "Seriously, though, Cassie. Stay safe. Message me when you get home, yeah?"

"Of course," I say, with a wink, "I wouldn't want my pretty kitty worrying."

Lori chuckles at my lame attempt to demonstrate an okay-ness with her Tech Shifting and waves her goodbyes as she pulls out onto the surprisingly quiet street. I *am* okay with knowing she Tech Shifts, especially as it's her primary way to de-stress. In a way, I'm lucky too; between Lori and the others at the regular meets up at the Forster Street Community Centre—who have all been really welcoming since I started intermittently, not to mention awkwardly, attending—my interactions with the Tech Shifting community has been pretty positive of late. Even the Kitsune case last month was fine in that respect. It was the non-TS crowd who caused all the trouble for me.

*Yet you still can't let go of the TS Murder Files, can you? No matter how different those around you are, you can't separate them in your head. Not completely.*

I shake away the bad thoughts and start making my way down Main Street. It would actually be a little quicker to take some of the back streets, but I'm guessing Lori brought up the muggings because the news sites have been reporting a sudden spike in them recently. She made a joke of it, but she really does worry, I can tell that much. Even if Lori can't see me doing it, I'd rather take the precautions to make sure she doesn't have to worry so much. So, Main Street with all its lights and public visibility it is.

It really is a nice night out, though, complete with a clear sky and a bright, shiny moon to look down on me. It's still early enough that the drinkers and the eternal partygoers aren't out in full swing yet, so it's pretty quiet too. In fact, for most of the walk, the loudest sound I can hear is the quiet *put-put-put* of the EU25s that line the kerb of the street at regular intervals. The idea of the small metal boxes is they sit nondescriptly just within the bounds of the kerb and process the air put out by the non-electric cars going up and down the road. I stop and lean down to watch the little machine in action because, well, despite my normal mixed emotions about some of our modern tech, these things fascinate me.

We were at one point expected to go entirely electric with vehicles, but it's still cheaper to run a car on fossil and biofuels, so the city is pretty evenly split in terms of who owns what. Even if biodiesel is still the higher seller of the two, it does emit an odour. Personally, I think biodiesel emissions smell a little like burnt fries, which isn't entirely unpleasant as car exhaust fumes go, but I get why people don't like it. The current thinking is that, now the poorly titled petroleum cloning research has started gaining ground, it's likely we'll see an influx of biodiesel cars within the next twenty years. You see, since the animal rights protests have died down in relation to cloning what are essentially modified but already dead animals in order to harvest unnatural amounts of fat to help produce the fuel, the *experts* are touting how the prices are going to drop again.

Which would mean more burnt fast food wafting through the streets. So, about two weeks ago, the Government rushed out the installation of the EnviroUnit version 25, or EU25, so they could road test it in a live environment. The machine takes in the emissions, neutralises the smell through some sort of techno-magic, and releases a virtually odourless equivalent in its stead. The general consensus so far is they're working really well. Not to mention they've had a positive effect on other potentially unwanted stinks; like mess left by the living animals who now only make up a little over a third of the city's pet population, or the liquid expulsions of those who can't tell when to stop drinking.

"No, these I can get on board with," I say, getting to my feet and continuing my journey.

"Help...me..."

I freeze. "Hello?"

"Help...me. Please..." the voice comes again, rising weakly from a darkened alley a few steps ahead.

I narrow my eyes, my internal paranoia engine on full alert. Mysterious voices crying for help from darkened alleys are not always what they seem. My moral compass is pointing due innocent-in-trouble, though, so I opt for the balanced approach and walk towards the alley. Slowly.

I give a quick glance around to make sure that my exits are clear and reply, "Hello? I can't see you. What happened?"

"Lured in...three men. Took my purse," the voice rasps, clearly female now, and carrying an air of a genuine struggle to get the words out with it.

I take a deep breath and make a decision there and then. "Okay, I'm coming in. Whereabouts are you?"

Silence.

I walk forward a few more steps, pushing through the contents of a flipped dumpster, and try again. "Miss? I can't see you."

"Back here. Bleeding. Help...me. Please."

It takes ten more steps for me to hear the alarm bells ringing in my head. *Help me. Please.* It sounded the same as the first time she said it. *Exactly* the same.

I turn to head back towards Main Street but realise very quickly that I'm too late. A bright flash of light hits my eyes and, before I can bring my hand up to shield my vision, my hands flinch back involuntarily as a wave of fear rushes over me. I stumble back, heading further into the alley as I try to escape, and trip over something on the floor. Or it may have been my own feet. I can't tell any more. My vision is blurring, and as each flash of light hits me, I see a figure getting closer and closer.

Something inside me registers what I'm looking at and I start to retch, my stomach forcing its contents up and out onto the ground in front of me. The warmth of it is pooling around my hands, bringing with it the realisation that I've somehow pushed myself up onto all fours. I force my head away from the light, but it makes no difference. I still can't see properly, can't even begin to get to my feet. And the voices; whispering incoherently from all around me.

Two gloved hands reach out and touch me. A voice in the back of my head screams, *Run! Get up and run!*

But I can't.

All I can do is whisper one word as I feel a tightness in my head, and the darkness engulfs my vision.

"Vampire."


COLD. I'M COLD. And if I can feel that, then I'm not dead. Or not yet anyway.

I open my eyes, but they immediately blink shut as soon as the light hits them. "Ow."

"Hey!" someone yells in the fading darkness. There's a bed underneath me. A crappy bed with a thin, broken mattress and a creaky frame that's rather rudely protesting my presence, but a bed nonetheless. "I think she's waking up."

I try to open my eyes again and push myself up into a sitting position, my hand instinctively reaching out to find a cold, hard wall to my right. I lean into it just as the sound of a heavy door slams open to my left.

"Get Sanderson back in here," a familiar, gruff voice grumps. Is it…?

"Hoove?" I manage. "That you?"

"Got it in one. Sit tight, Caz. Someone get her some water."

My vision starts to come back enough for me to begin to pick out a few details in my surroundings. Muted, plain walls. A bed that was probably dumped somewhere. Heavyweight door with a movable, and currently open, viewing hatch. "You wanna tell me why I'm in a cell?"

Captain Hoover takes a bottle of water from someone I don't recognise and thrusts it towards me. "A lot of reasons. We'll get to that, though. First things first, drink this."

I do as I'm told and the person who brought the water squats down in front of me. He looks concerned. "Miss Tam, I'm Doctor Sanderson. I'm afraid you've had a bit of a...well, let's just say, *an experience.* I need to check you over, is that okay?"

I nod my consent and the apparent doctor starts giving me a very basic physical while asking a few questions he doesn't really want answers to. "Do you remember what happened to you? Don't tell me what, I just need to know if you have *any* recollection at all."

*Weird that he doesn't want the details. Roll with it, Tam. You'll get some answers eventually.* "Bits and pieces. It all felt kinda jumpy when it happened."

"Okay, good. No history of epilepsy? Or generalised light sensitivity?"

"No, and no."

"Any illnesses recently? I mean anything, even a mild cold."

"No."

"Excellent. Can you lean your head forward, please? And move your hair?"

I lean forward and sweep my hair to the side, and Doctor Sanderson lifts a small device up to the back of my neck. It reminds me of those tiny torches opticians sometimes use. It makes a little beep, and he pulls it back. I glance up to see him studying what I'm assuming is a small readout on the top of the stick-like device. "Functioning," he says. "You may sit up now."

I tilt my head back and push my hair back over my shoulders, making a point of running my fingers over where the doctor was using his beeping machine. When I find the two puncture wounds, one scabbed over, and the other closed but bulging slightly, my blood runs cold, and my eyes go wide. Hoove is staring at me, not unsympathetically, while Sanderson keeps talking.

"She's either not one of those targeted with the proteins, or she didn't have enough exposure. You're lucky."

The burly Captain of the New Hopeland PD nods and gives his thick moustache a thoughtful stroke. Finally, he says, "Is she going to be okay with this?"

Sanderson glances at me, turns back to Hoove, and shrugs. "Physically she'll be fine, bar the expected risks with what you're planning. Emotionally? She's responsive, but you know her better than I do."

"Tough as old boots," Hoove replies with a smile. "And far too stubborn to make this easy. Okay, Caz. You better come with me."

I nod and rise to my feet. I'm a little shaky, but not as bad as I expected. As we walk, I notice that the denizens of the station are paying a larger than normal amount of attention to me. Most look either curious or wary. When we pass Corporal Devereux and Lieutenant Hanson huddled together over a desk, they shoot me a concerned look and turn to Hoove. He nods, and their shoulders sag, relief drifting over their faces, but not quite masking the lingering worry. *Why do I get the feeling this isn't going to be my favourite conversation with the leader of New Hopeland's finest?*

We make a brief stop at the staff toilets because, well, I can still smell the vomit on me. I appreciate that someone obviously wiped me down a little before dumping me in the cell, but there's nothing like a therapeutic assault of cheap hand soap and lukewarm water in your face to...okay, so it doesn't actually do much at all. But it's all I've got at my disposal right now. The slightly damp, abandoned hair tie I found on the sink is also useful at this point, if for no other reason than that I'm now hyperaware of every time my hair brushes the marks on the back of my neck. A rather stiff twist of said body part reveals little more than a couple of dark marks. Damn positioning. I give my face another splash and head back out to the main station.

Finally, we reach a door with "Captain A. Hoover" written on the window in block lettering. We enter and my unusually quiet escort waves me to a nice, padded chair at the front, then immediately heads over to his personal percolator. From how steaming hot it looks, I'll assume he had someone fill it while he was waiting for me. He grabs two mugs and fills them black. I'd rather a double-double at this point, but I'll take whatever caffeine I can get. I have no idea what blend he's using, but the scent is enough to jolt me awake a little more. I push the mug aside to cool and take another swig from my depleted water bottle instead.

"So," Hoove says.

"So."

"I know you've probably got a lot of questions right now, and to be honest with you, Caz, I don't even know where to begin with this."

I sigh and decide to play nice. "I guess we start at the beginning. How about I tell you what I remember, and we move on from there?" Hoove nods and I continue, "I was walking home, heading south down Main Street. I'd come from Cartwright's, a café up on Dunstone Avenue, and must have been about halfway down, I think? It can't have been much later than maybe quarter past nine. I stopped to look at one of the EU25s and..."

"Was there a reason you stopped? Anything suspicious?" Hoove interjects, and I shake my head.

"I just like them. Look, Hoove, my memory is a bit hazy. I know it's not really protocol, but do ya think you could hold off on the questions until I get through what springs to mind? Let me try to work through it all before you start nudging me, eh?"

Hoover sits back into his chair and grins. I can't think there are many who would talk to him like I sometimes do. He's approachable enough, but he demands respect, and most of his staff give it to him freely. I'm not staff, though. "Go ahead," he replies.

"So, I hear a voice coming from down an alley, calling for help. I can't remember which alley, but I'd guess you guys know. It was a woman's voice, saying she'd been mugged by three men and she was bleeding. I got about halfway down there when I realised some of the stuff she'd said, she'd repeated in the exact same tone, like it was a recording. I turned to leave, and that was when I got attacked. This is where it all gets a bit weird. There was this bright light flashing in my eyes, and I started feeling dizzy, and off balance. Then, there was this *fear* that washed over me and ..."

I freeze, eyes wide, and Hoove leans forward again. "You okay? Do you need some more time?"

I blink, shake my head, and make a grab for the coffee. It's still too hot, but the slight burn as it runs down my throat helps, in a way. "No. No, I'll keep going. There were voices. They were sort of chattering, I guess. I couldn't really make them out. Uh, this *person* was walking towards me. I passed out just after they touched me. It's weird, though. I mean, the whole thing is weird, but the way they moved...it could have been the way the light flashed, but they had this sort of smooth *lope* to them. But they were all over the place, moving side to side. I couldn't track them properly. And the way they looked. It was odd. I can't quite..."

I trail off again and start staring at the wall at the back of the room. I can see the person in my mind, but I can't seem to get the words out.

The silence hangs in the air for a few seconds, and my brow furrows.

"Let me try," Hoove cuts in, his voice deep but gentle. "Dressed all in a shiny, black, skintight material. They wore boots, and gloves that made their fingers look elongated. You couldn't see their face because they wore a helmet of some sort. It had a long visor covering the entire face, other than two long sections at the bottom that seemed to glow. It was smooth, had two protrusions on the side looking kinda like ears, and the number forty-eight was printed at the top where the forehead should be."

I nod. "Yeah. I can't give you any more than that, because it was too dark. Or too light. The helmet, though. I mean, I didn't really notice the number on it, but it... It made think of an old film. *Nosferatu?*" I realise I'm stroking the marks on my neck again and force my hand back onto the desk with a slap. "I sound crazy, even to me, but I just kept thinking..." I swallow hard. "Vampire."

Captain Hoover drops his chin onto his hand and says, "Sounds about right."

*Ah, now that reaction tells me a lot.* I take another mouthful of coffee and ask, "I'm not the first victim, am I?"

"No."

"How many attacks have there been?"

"Too many. I'm glad you remember what you do. If you hadn't, that would have potentially made this a lot more difficult, on a number of levels."

"How so? Has this got something to do with what the doc was saying about—what was it, proteins?"

There's an old interview where the reporter accidentally said Captain Hoo-Haa instead of Captain Hoover when making his introductions. Hoove was unable to stop himself reacting and ended up wrinkling his nose like he'd just realised the guy hadn't washed for a month. He's pulling the same face now.

"It's all crackpot conspiracy theory stuff. You ever hear of optogenetics?" I shake my head, and he continues, "It's the study of how light affects neurons or something. He thinks that, as none of the victims can remember every little detail, whoever's behind this has been targeting specific people and flooding their water supply with light-sensitive proteins carried in viruses. That way, the light these people are using causes a partial memory loss and stops them getting caught."

"But you don't think that's the case."

"No. There's no evidence to support the theory in terms of illness or the handful of DNA tests he's done. Plus, we've been looking, and there's nothing to link the various victims yet. This is more likely opportunistic. He won't drop it, though, so I've given up calling him on the theory. To be quite frank, as long as we get useful information out of his checks, he can chase dead ends all he wants."

"Opportunistic, eh? In a normal robbery, sure. But this is a real weird way to mug someone."

"It would be, if these were straightforward muggings. I'll get you to check later, but I don't think you'll find any personal items missing. In all the previous attacks, only one thing has been taken. I'll give you a clue what: what do vampires take?"

"Blood."

"Exactly."

I narrow my eyes. "You're being awfully open about all of this. It's not that I don't appreciate it, but you shouldn't be telling me everything you are."

"Of course I should. Why wouldn't I share pertinent information with an investigating officer? I've gotta keep you all up to date, right?"

"Investigating...? Hoove, I like working with you guys and all, but I'm a victim here," I snap, rising to my feet.

"Sit down, Caz."

His tone is firm, but much like the looks he was giving me back in the cell, it isn't unsympathetic. So I comply, albeit with an added grumpy sneer and an exaggerated crossing of my arms. "I'm not going to like this, am I?"

A weariness crosses the Captain's face. He sighs and says, "Remember the little joyride you took last month?"

"When I delivered the proven criminal to you, prevented a potential incident that would have caused mass panic, and saved you all a load of work, you mean?"

"Now, don't think it ain't appreciated, Caz, but here's the thing. *My* bosses have been breathing down my neck about you ever since that mess with the Eddie Redwood case. As soon as they found out, and don't ask me how they did, that you tore through the city, not to mention the gunfight and collateral damage along the way, they started pushing for me to bring you in and revoke your investigation licence. I've been arguing with them, making excuses, but I've gotta be honest with ya here, I was running out of ideas. When you got dragged in with those marks on your neck, and the other little thing I'll show you in a minute, it gave me an out. Whether you like it or not, you've got two choices at this point. Go along with what I'm gonna tell you, or head back to the cells and start your journey along the career change path. I don't want to be doing this, Caz, but I'll like it even less if you pick the latter."

"*Diu.* You can't be serious."

"Do I look like I'm joking?" he asks, and I can see the anger burning behind his eyes. It isn't aimed at me, even though I've put myself—and in turn, him—in this position, though, that much is clear.

I groan and rub my eyes, then grump, "I guess I don't really have a choice, do I?"

Hoove lets out a sigh of relief, and states, simply, "Thank fuck for that." He picks up his phone and dials a couple of digits. "Get everyone in here. We're good to go."

WITHIN SECONDS, THE room is a lot fuller. In a way, it's almost a relief to see Corporal Devereux and Lieutenant Hanson walk in, even if Hanson's playful ruffling of my hair sets off a momentary headache.

I don't recognise the other newcomer, though. He's got an almost arrogant air to him, like a boxer who's turning up the showmanship in his stance to play to the crowd. Judging by the rubber-tipped plugs running down his shaven head, he's part of the New Hopeland PD's Tech Shifter Division. "Cassandra Tam," he says, his voice dripping with a gruff, but recognisably Irish lilt. "I didn't get to introduce m'self the last time you were helping *us* out."

The man shuts his mouth and, obviously used to this, Hoove carries out the introduction. "This is Donal O'Brien, current Marshal of the TS Division. He's a hybrid wolf, if you were wondering. Given the circumstances, I'm sure you can understand why we're making use of Donal's skill set."

*Donal O'Brien,* I repeat to myself, being careful to maintain my poker face. *The emphasis on* us *was for* my *benefit. Does that mean this is related to the Kings? Or Fuerza? Well, isn't that just great.* "A pleasure," I reply.

"If you hadn't guessed," Captain Hoover continues, "Caz has agreed to help us out. There's a lot she doesn't know yet..."

"Like the plan," Hanson cuts in. "You know, seeing as the windows are intact and you don't have a black eye and all."

"Thank you, Lieutenant Hanson. Nothing builds trust quite like creating a feeling of dread, does it?"

"I certainly think so," she smirks.

Hoove gives her a dissatisfied snort and pulls open a drawer on his side of the desk. He retrieves a small, plastic bag and passes it to me. "What would you say this is?"

I twist the bag a few times, studying its contents. "Looks like a small vial of some sort. It's broken, obviously. Given what we've been discussing, I'm gonna guess that the red stains are blood."

"Your blood to be precise," Donal says. "You've helped blow the case right open."

"Explain."

"The attacker was interrupted," Corporal Devereux says. "We got an anonymous call confirming that someone had been attacked in an alley and they were unconscious. By the time I got there, the caller was gone, and you were...not in a good way. The vial was lying right next to you. We checked, and it was a match for you."

"Before we picked you up," Hanson adds, "all we knew for sure was the attacker was implanting trackers in their victims. *This* gave us the tip-off that they were taking blood."

My hand goes to the bump under my skin, and I frown. "Trackers?"

Hanson raises her eyebrows at her Captain and asks, "Seriously? You hadn't told her?"

"Yeah, seriously?" I echo. "You hadn't told me?"

"We were getting to it," Hoove responds, undeterred. "See, we managed to give one of them a look-over on another victim. They give out a clear signal; it's definitely an identification of some sort, but it isn't sent anywhere other than *out*. Most likely answer is that it can be picked up by the attacker if they come near one. Whether that's to avoid duplicate attacks or to make them easier, we don't know."

"Removal's easy enough," Hanson says, tilting her head to show me a small scar. "Local anaesthetic, slice, done."

I note Hanson's attack in the file marked "question later" and ask, "And you're gonna get it out of me too, right?"

"Eventually," Donal laughs, and I reel on him.

"And what the hell is *that* supposed to mean?" I turn back to my temporary boss and repeat, "You're gonna get it out of me. Right?"

Captain Hoover sniffs and reaches into what I'm now dubbing his "drawer of increasingly inconvenient wonders" and pulls out a small wad of papers. He pushes them towards me so that I can shuffle through them. "Based on a combination of known timings and the medical checks Doctor Sanderson has been carrying out, the actual attacks don't last long. The lighting makes it difficult to catch anything close to a clear photo of the attacker too. The second to last sheet is the best we've got."

"A dark blur," I huff.

"Pretty much. We zoomed in on the hands, though. Have a look at the second photo and tell me what you see."

I study the photo for a few seconds, then chuck it back on the table and throw my hands out in defeat. "A glove. Something's reflecting off it. Or a small section of it. What about it?"

"The size of the reflection," Corporal Devereaux confirms, "is consistent with a single vial, like the one we recovered from where you were attacked."

"And how exactly do you know that?"

"We recreated it," he replies. "Don't worry, we'll show you how later if you want to see. The main thing is it does mean that, for whatever reason, the attacker is only stealing a small amount of blood from each victim."

A few puzzle pieces start to fall in place. I haven't got the full picture yet, but I can see enough to know what's coming. "Even if we're working on the idea that the attacks are opportunistic in nature...it doesn't matter if the tracker is there to avoid double attacks or make them more likely. If the attacker is only taking small samples, the fact they failed with me means they'll likely try again." I turn back to Hoove and give him an incredulous look. "You want to use me as bait!"

Hoove stares at me for a moment, thinks better of trying to wrap it up in fancy words, and replies, "That's about the size of it."

"Oh, come on! Is that why you put me in a cell? So you can still go with the plan, even if I didn't agree to it?"

"No, that was my fault," Hanson says. "The attack affects different people in different ways. Nausea and fear are common, as is the passing out. When you come to, though, it starts to get a bit mixed up. We've had continued blurred vision, near catatonia... I *may* have been a little, uhm, aggressive. We figured a safe environment would be good regardless of how you reacted, but the idea of using the cell mostly came up because people were worried you'd react how I did. Sorry about that."

My head drops, and I rub my eyes. "I can't believe this."

"Believe it, Caz. Right now, if we want to prevent more attacks, you're the best shot we have."

I take a deep breath to centre myself. "Okay," I sigh. "Okay. But I need to know *everything*. Starting with anything you've figured out about how this person carries out the attacks."

"Devereaux," Hoove says with a nod. "Take Caz and show her what we're working with. O'Brien, go check how the modifications to your face are going. And, Hanson?"

"Yes, Captain?"

"You're with me. Since your mouth has been running near non-stop today, you can do the paperwork to make Caz an official part of this investigation."

"Paperwork? Oh, joy," she laughs.

"Dismissed."


WE ALL FILE out of Captain Hoover's office, with the exception of Lieutenant Hanson and the Captain himself. Donal gives me a firm pat on the back that causes me to stumble more than I would have liked. "Aftereffects are a bitch. Catch ya later," he says and heads off towards the elevator down to the TS storage and repair room under the station.

Corporal Devereaux nods up a hallway and I follow obediently. He slows to match my pace and says quietly, "Don't discuss anything out here. Wait until we're in the war room."

I remain silent, which Devereaux takes as an agreement, and we keep moving towards the back of the police station. The layout of the place has always interested me. New buildings have popped up in New Hopeland, usually in empty spaces that were allocated for future developments, but much of the original architecture remains. The early buildings fit into two categories. The most common can broadly be described as generic but modern-at-the-time areas set aside for incoming businesses and residences. The other ones, like this station, were specially designed for a specific purpose. What it means in this case is when you enter the building, you can see the entrance to the main offices at the back of the public area, raised slightly but set in the centre. On either side sits a corridor.

If you're facing towards the offices, the left wall of the left-hand corridor is lined with cells. There's also a clear cut-off wall at the end. On the right-hand corridor, which is where we're heading, the right wall is lined with a couple of recreational areas until about halfway down. Then come the general meeting rooms, used primarily for daily rundowns, interviews, and non-priority cases, and a small number of dedicated war rooms set aside for larger operations. Where things get interesting for me is that, once you hit the end of the right-hand corridor, there's a left turn, taking you behind the office area. Here, you'll find nothing but a ramp heading down into the lower levels of the station.

The reason this interests me is there is nothing in these purpose-built buildings that wasn't pegged for what was deemed to be a necessary function. When I helped out with the TS Murder Files, the weapons storage facility was at the bottom of the first ramp. The second ramp went down another floor to the area Donal O'Brien is currently heading for. It's an important space because, while a couple of humans can fit into the elevator to get down there, hybrid-style Tech Shifter gear adds a fair bit of length to the user's legs. The same can be said of the full animal suits as both styles use the same stilt setup to improve appearance and balance, but it's only the hybrids who have trouble with the height of doors as a result.

Even if you put aside the possibility the PD were already looking at forming a TS division during those cases, the station has still been around for a lot longer than Tech Shifting has existed. That area *must* have been used for something before Donal and his team came onto the scene, but I don't know what. And for that matter, if it was so important it needed a dedicated area when the station was opened, where has whatever was going on down there gone now? Was it no longer needed? Was there enough spare space to keep it going? Is there another floor? These are all questions I've asked before, but the usual answers I get are either "I don't know," or "You don't need to know." Curiosity damn near killed the Caz, though, so I don't do any more than occasionally nudge people in the hope they'll tell me. As it is, I'm still in the dark.

We enter the darkened war room at the end of the hall, leaving the mystery ramp tantalisingly in view, and Devereaux flicks a light switch. Once everything has been illuminated, I'm quite taken aback. The map on the wall immediately catches my eye. When I stroll over and do a quick count, the enormity of what we're facing suddenly becomes apparent. "I see seventeen attacks in the city."

"Eighteen," Devereaux corrects, placing a new marker in an alley on Main Street.

I shiver. "How have I not heard anything about this before?"

"You've heard about the recent increase in muggings, eh?"

I turn to Devereaux and frown. "A cover-up?"

"Yeah. It has its own problems, though. You know what this city's like. People hear there are more muggings, and they start to try their luck."

"So, you've created your own crime epidemic."

"It's...easier to control that way."

I can tell from his tone that Devereaux is repeating the official stance on the PD's actions, but he isn't entirely convinced it's the right way to handle it all. I'm mixed on the whole thing, but years of navigating the wasp nest that is New Hopeland have taught me how important it is to hide some things. Life here is like a game of cards; you bluff and manipulate until, by fair means or foul, you have a winning hand. "Muggings are familiar to people, so while knowing there's a spate of them will be scary for people, it's a lot less scary than what we're *actually* dealing with. Plus, if it's blood that's being taken, it kinda *is* a mugging."

"Yeah," he replies, but he's still not entirely buying it.

I'm beginning to like Corporal Devereaux a lot more. In a way, he reminds me of me when I was back in Vancouver. He's not been corrupted by the system yet, and the way he's acting, he likely won't be, not to any great degree. It's just a shame that'll damage his career mobility.

"I can guess it's pretty easy to tell which cases are actual muggings and which are part of *this*," I say, waving at the map. "But what about the victims?"

"Doctor Sanderson treats all of them. He tells the majority of them they had traces of psychotropic drugs in their system which likely caused hallucinations. Drop in a few similar but false descriptors from alleged similar cases— black hair and clothes, oversized dark glasses and so on— and people start to believe it."

"Mass misdirection. Okay, so have there been any cases it didn't work in?"

"One or two, but we've been monitoring the situation and they all start to disbelieve their memories after a day or two. Our explanation makes more sense, even if it's fabricated."

I nod, walk over to a chair, and drop myself down with a sigh. "I can't deny that. What about the trackers?"

"They're small enough that we can tell most people they're just shrapnel from the surrounding area or the attacker's weapon. Doctor Sanderson gives them some antibiotics—placebos—and says they'll work their own way out, but if they don't come out within two weeks, to come and see him again and he'll remove them. He's removed three so far, not including Hanson's."

"So, four then. If he's getting them to leave it two weeks...that's a lot of attacks in a relatively short space of time."

"Yeah. There's never more than a day or two between attacks. Sometimes, it's an attack every night for a short burst. It's been a busy three weeks."

"I bet." I lean back into my chair and ask, "So, what do we do know that I haven't been told yet?"

"Honestly?" Devereaux pulls up a chair of his own. "Not much. Everything's theoretical at the moment."

"I get that, but I'm still gonna need to be caught up. Like this vial thing. How did you recreate it?"

"That's interesting actually. Okay, training academy 101. What do you know about non-lethal weapons?"

I shoot Devereaux a wicked grin and reply, "There are none, Will. All weapons are lethal if you use them right."

"They must have loved you in training," he laughs. "Seriously, though, what can you remember?"

"That non-lethals are the preference in most situations. Or, that's the official line as far as the public is concerned anyway. To be honest with you, I was booted out before I could spend too much time with them, so my knowledge of standard-issue weaponry mostly extends to stuff I was able to replace with similar items when I started out as a PI. Which means guns. Funny, eh? The police preach about the use of non-lethal weapons, but the ones readily available to the public fall into the lethal category."

"Sad but true. Okay, so do you know what LED Incapacitators are?"

"Light-based tools designed to subdue."

"Correct. They work kinda like flashlights, but rather than a gentle illumination, they send out bright, rapid pulses in different colours. The idea is the changes are so quick that human eyes can't adapt, causing intracranial pressure..."

"Intracranial pressure?" I cut in.

Devereaux taps his head and clarifies, "Pressure inside the skull. It feels like it's right inside your brain. Anyway, it causes a lot of grief for targets; severe headaches, nausea, vomiting, disorientation, irritability, and temporary blindness are the most commonly reported."

"Which sounds a lot like what I experienced."

"And a lot like what other victims have experienced too."

"So the light I saw *has* to have been adapted from an LED Incapacitator, then."

"That's what I thought. I think the only reason no one else thought of it is they've all been out of the academy a lot longer than me here. And, as you said, the preference for non-lethal weapons is a public-facing façade. Don't get me wrong, it's a necessity in a city like this, but it means no one really thought along those lines to start with. When I brought it up, Lieutenant Hanson raised a good point. LED Incapacitators are inconsistent."

"Inconsistent, how?"

"The effect they have on targets is quite varied. The list I gave you wouldn't all apply to one person in every case. In fact, in some cases, they don't work at all."

"Which, given the frequency of attacks, means there was the possibility the attacker would have already come across at least one victim who was unaffected."

"Exactly. So, Lieutenant Hanson pointed out that LED Incapacitators technically fall under the category of Dazzlers. The weapons all use laser-based lighting operating in different areas of the electromagnetic spectrum, though. When used on humans, most Dazzlers either work with a red laser diode or a green diode-pumped solid-state laser. Historically, the green light models have been more consistently effective than the LED Incapacitators."

"If you're telling me about both, then it means the broader Dazzlers don't entirely fit either, do they?"

Devereaux nods. "Dazzlers are designed to cause temporary blindness and disorientation, but nothing else."

"Makes the Doc's optogenetics thingy sound more plausible, doesn't it?" Lieutenant Hanson says, sliding in through the door.

"Aren't you supposed to be doing paperwork?" I ask, raising my eyebrows at her.

"Yup," she replies with a grin and pulls a chair up next to Corporal Devereaux. "Dev told you there was no evidence for the protein virus theory, right?"

I fight to suppress a smile at Devereaux wincing at Hanson's nickname for him. She told me once that she only shortens his name to Dev because she knows he hates it. "No, but Hoove did. So, if neither fits entirely, what are we thinking?"

"I thought it may be a combo," Devereaux says. "Like a linked-up system of light disruption."

"Hoover said you made the vampire connection," Hanson adds. "Do you know why?"

"Not really," I concede. "It makes sense now I know about the blood-taking, but there was *something* about their helmet that made me think it. I just can't quite pinpoint what."

Hanson nods. "A couple of the victims described large fang-shaped protrusions at the base of the helmet. The design was probably intentional, to evoke that particular image. Nothing like being sent back to fearing the monsters under the bed to cause panic, right?"

"My theory," Devereaux says, "is one *fang* is an LED Incapacitator, and the other is a different type of Dazzler. They work in tandem, with the Dazzler making the initial hit due to consistency, then the LED Incapacitator joining in afterward once the victim is already feeling the effects."

I nod. "That makes sense. So, how does this fit with you knowing it was a vial in the photo?"

"We've had the light theory since around attack ten or eleven, but we've had the photo longer. Our initial thinking was it was simply a control system that had become exposed on the glove, but it seemed a little small for that. Once we retrieved the vial from you, though, Lieutenant Hanson made a possible connection."

"I grabbed a spare vial from Doc Sanderson, stuck it to a glove, turned the lights off, and waved my hand in front of a high-power torch held under my chin." Hanson shrugs. "The effect was close enough to confirm it."

"I felt it touch my neck," I grunt. "The glove takes the blood and implants the tracker."

"Looks that way," Hanson replies and gets to her feet. "Well, I better get back up there before the good Captain misses me. I'm glad you're okay, Cassie. If you need to borrow a top or anything before you leave, let me know."

# Chapter Two

BY THE TIME I leave the station, we're heading into the afternoon. I could have technically left sooner, but Corporal Devereaux offered to take my official statement before I headed up to finalise the paperwork. While that made for delays in my exit, I was gonna have to do it sooner or later, and I'd rather get it all done in one go than have to come back in later. The paperwork itself was easy enough. My terms were pretty much the same as when I worked the TS Murder Files; full pay for the duration, expenses covered, and access to police resources within reason and with suitable supervision. I took Hanson up on her offer of borrowing a top too. She's better toned than I am but muscular enough that the sleeves fit me fine, even if the top itself is half a size too small. I don't recognise the logo on it, but from the text, I'd guess it belongs to an Australian brewery. I mean, what else would a kangaroo drinking a can of lager and giving a thumbs-up be?

Scanning my phone reveals I have two missed calls, both expected. The first is from Lori, no doubt checking I really did get home safely. The other is from the offices of Familiar Enterprises Ltd. I was due to visit them at half nine this morning, and their call will have been to ask where exactly I was. Luckily, the CEO of the company, Jonah Burrell, is fairly understanding when it comes to me. He once hired me to find his kidnapped daughter, reasoning that getting the police involved would make the mess far more public than I would. And find her I did, in the arms of her lover. As it transpired, she had faked her kidnapping to be with the guy. Unfortunately for her, she wasn't the only dishonest one in the affair, as her *lover* had intended to use the ransom money to buy out a majority share in FE Ltd and usurp her father's power base. Long story short, he was very grateful, even if it did hit the news sites in the end, and he provided me with an otherwise far-out-of-my-price-range luxury item in return: Bert, my gargoyle-esque Familiar Unit.

I respond to Lori first. She'll be working right now, helping to cover today's political open house question session, so I don't want to disturb her too much. So, instead of calling, I drop her a quick message.

*Sorry, something happened that made calling difficult. I'll explain later. Wanna drop by mine around eight?*

I stop outside my apartment block and return the call to FE Ltd. The answering voice is that of a bored-sounding receptionist. "Welcome to Familiar Enterprises Limited. My name is Brenda, how can I help?"

"Hi, Brenda, I was just returning a call from earlier. I know what it's about, I had an appointment at half nine, but I missed it."

"By quite a margin," she yawns. "Can you confirm your name and the name of the person you had the appointment with please?"

"Sure. My name's Cassandra Tam. The appointment was originally with Jonah Burrell, but he said he'd be farming it out to one of the techs. I didn't get confirmation of the name."

Brenda tuts down the phone and replies, "Sounds about right. Men. You can't live with them, you can't throw them in a river and drown them. Ah well. You were due to consult with a Mrs. Faraday. She has some time free at three today if that would be suitable?"

"Yes! Definitely! Sorry to be a pain, Brenda, but do the original notes state whether I need to bring my Familiar Unit with me?"

"Uhm…no, they don't. Would you like me to check?"

"Yes, please."

"Please hold."

The line cuts to hold music. Some companies have a pretty good selection going in that department. A bank I had to call on a case last week even gave the option of choosing my hold music by genre. FE Ltd, it seems, is not one of these companies. Instead, I'm treated to what I can only assume is "Elevator Music Classics Volume One, as performed by one person with a songbook and a high school quality keyboard." Thankfully, Brenda cuts in partway through a rendition of something that may have been Elvis but could just have easily been Marilyn Manson.

"Mrs. Faraday says that, in light of how recent your Unit's last maintenance check was, there's no need. If it turns out to require urgent attention, she can simply summon it or arrange a pickup."

"Okay, thank you, Brenda."

"You're welcome. Have a nice day."

And with that, my call is cut short. *Well, that was easy.*

My phone lights up again, just as I start to push it into my pocket. I smile when I see it's a reply from Lori.

*Sounds good. I'll bring doughnuts.*

I hit reply but can't think of anything cool sounding to send back, so go with a stock *Great. See you then.* Yup, lame, generic texts are my middle name.

"Well," I tell myself. "That gives you time to shower and check through the stuff Devereaux's sending you."


BERT IS CLEARLY less than pleased about my unannounced overnight absence. I can tell, because the moment I open the door, he clambers up onto my work table and half closes the metal rings at the top of his eyes to make it look like he's glaring at me. He then proceeds to run a flexibility test on his left foot claws, essentially drumming his nails on the table. "Caw," he says.

"Don't ask," I reply. "Let's just say that I'm perfectly capable of getting in trouble without trying at the moment."

Bert relaxes his eyes and lowers himself off the table with a *clunk*. He makes his way over to the kitchen and clambers up the side of the worktop to take position where his charger is currently situated. I take the hint, pull the chord out of the wall plug, and slide one of his back panels aside so I can click it into place. Bert's body relaxes into the statue-like squat that is his "off" pose. Charging should take between six and eight hours, depending on how much battery he's spent while I've been out. Given the lack of visible damage I can see, he obviously wasn't too bored, so that's something.

With the metal menace shut down, I'm free to clean up uninhibited by anything other than my own self-imposed time constraints. First things first, though. I tap the voice command button at the bottom of the tablet sitting on my work desk, and the screen flickers into life. The wall-mounted speakers immediately state, "Good afternoon, Cassandra. How may I be of assistance?"

"Email check. Sender, Devereaux."

"Please wait... You have one unread message matching this criterion."

"Any attachments?"

"Zero attachments detected. Scan indicates that message contains a secure gateway to an isolated file storage system."

"Is it a police storage system?"

"Data indicates that storage system belongs to New Hopeland Police Department. Access is restricted without gateway use."

"Okay. Set up new subfolder. Destination server six, open case files. New folder title, 'Orlok,' spelling O-R-L-O-K. Confirm when action complete."

"Please wait... Complete."

"Copy contents of gateway storage system to Orlok. Once complete, store gateway access point in Orlok, set synch settings to automatically scan for altered and new files in gateway storage, and copy to Orlok. Set file settings in the folder to store previous versions until told otherwise. Once complete, run test and, if successful, securely delete the email containing the gateway."

"Please wait... Process may take some time."

I nod at the screen, not that it can see me, and add, "Please confirm when complete. Change settings to single room audio. Tracking mode target, Cassandra Tam."

"Settings confirmed."

With the tablet busily working through the police files, I make my way to the shower cubicle in my bathroom. I strip out of my clothes, step inside, and turn the dial, letting a hard blast of water run over my face and into my auburn hair. I told Lori about the manual control system I have installed, complete with my reasoning about not trusting solid-state computers to understand that different days may mean I have different preferences when it comes to comfortable temperatures. She laughed and agreed that non-AI machines, whether solid-state or vintage fan-based in nature, wouldn't have any temperature focused empathy, simulated or otherwise. She still chalked it up to my mildly contradictory feelings about the pros and cons of how technologically reliant we're becoming as a species, though. I picture the bemused grin Lori gave me after that one, and a smile creeps up onto my own face. Unfortunately, it's short-lived.

As the warmth of the water cascades over me, I finally notice I've been on high alert all day. Something inside me had obviously reverted to my default work state the moment it realised I was still alive. I know this because my body is starting to relax a little. Cramps and muscle tightness I wasn't aware of are warming up, and slowly fading into something closer to a tired stiffness. Feeling like I do now, I'm grateful for the way my body reacts to things. Had I not developed this ability to block everything out and drown myself in stubborn detachment, there's no way I would have made it back here unaided.

Slowly, I turn my back to the shower spray and drop into a sitting position, my head bowed against the raised legs I'm now clutching tightly. Even with the hot water pouring over me, even with the loud *pitter-patter* of it hitting both my body and the bottom of the cubicle, I can hear my sobs and feel the warm tears rolling down my cheeks. It doesn't matter that I still can't remember everything that happened, because the most important thing is still lingering in the back of my mind. Fear. I was afraid. And I'm still afraid now, maybe even more so, because I've agreed to *let* myself get attacked again. The sound of the shower fades away, leaving me alone with my tears and the chattering voices echoing around the alley in my mind.

The silent water catches the bump where the tracker in my neck is placed, and it begins to itch. Well, not really, I *know* it's psychosomatic, but that doesn't stop it feeling like it's trying to burrow its way out of my skin. I dig my nails into my legs, but the short snap of pain is secondary to the memory of fear washing over me.

"Synchronisation complete."

And just like that, I raise my head to look in the direction of the room speakers. My work façade doesn't fall back into place, not completely, but the momentary distraction is enough to snap me out of whatever had a hold of me. "They weren't trying to kill me," I tell myself, my brow furrowing into a frown as I take in the normal sounds around me.

I shake my head and cup my hands to collect some water from the bottom of the cubicle to splash in my face. I rise to my feet, grab the shower gel, and lather it up, then give myself a quick but thorough wash before shutting the dial off and grabbing a towel. Doing my best not to slip while lifting one leg to dry the foot at the bottom, I say, "Computer, open server six, primary folder case files, subfolder Orlok, and create a new folder titled 'personal notes.' Designate setting do not synchronise."

"Please wait... Test complete. Folder created, synchronisation confirmed as disabled."

I finish drying my body and wrap the towel around my hair, then say, "Open folder personal notes and create new file. Activate dictation."

"Dictation activated, please confirm text."

I take a deep breath and begin, "The attacker did not want to kill me. Though I did not know this during the actual attack, it is now clear that the aim was to take a sample of blood and nothing more. While the experience justifies the fear during the attack, knowing my life was not in clear danger now should negate the fear resurfacing. But it doesn't. Just thinking about it brings the fear back to the forefront. What confuses me is I've been in worse situations and, not only have I not felt the same level of fear during the events in question, knowing my life was truly in danger hasn't had the same effect on me in the aftermath.

"Part of me wonders if it's the similarities with *Nosferatu* that's to blame. Just as Tech Shifting brought the werewolves of old horror movies into reality, this has done the same with vampires. Even then, even with my intermittent discomfort around certain aspects of the Tech Shifting community, I don't get the same fear, and these are modern-day monsters that not only killed, but did so brutally. No, something else happened here. Maybe this is simply the way the vamp's light show hit me. Maybe we're missing something. Right now, the only thing I know for sure is I'm scared, and I want to catch this person as soon as possible. End dictation and save, file name notes."

"File saved."

I spend the rest of the next half hour drying my hair and deciding on an outfit. I'd normally head to FE Ltd in my work clothes, but it seems silly to do so when I'm just going to change once I get home again. Instead, I pick out a long-sleeve white shirt with a black tribal print on the front, and a blue pair of what is as close as I get to skinny jeans. A clean pair of trainers and an imitation leather jacket completes the ensemble. It takes me until I've left the building to realise that this *may* be the exact same outfit I wore to the cinema two weeks ago. In which case, I *may* have subconsciously picked it out because Lori complimented me in it last time.

"Screw it," I tell myself, as I head out towards a nearby cab. "You're not changing just because your girlfriend's opinion factored into your clothing choice. Enjoy someone thinking you look good and get on with it. Hi, is this cab free, or are you waiting for someone?"


FAMILIAR ENTERPRISES LTD was built on the back of a single product: The Familiar Unit. Designed to be the modern world's pet, the little beasties are robust, offer plenty of customisation in appearance and design, and don't require the same level of attention as a flesh and blood animal. Powered by an extremely talented multi-specialty team, FE Ltd rose up to offer an alternative to the old world's favourite companions, and in doing so, became an instant success.

Or that's what the tourist brochures say anyway. The truth is, it began life as six small but very different companies working on everything from children's toys to cell phone apps that utilise a toned-down version of Artificial Intelligence to prioritise tasks and make entertainment suggestions. Yes, the name of the company was based purely on one product, but the unremarkably limited success of the foundations doesn't make for as feel-good a story when the tourists come for the guided tour. Of course, the past is not the only thing visitors don't see.

These particular offices are really nice. They're modern, fancy, and everything is compartmentalised in a logical manner. The tours take you through the public screening room with its wall-to-wall screens showing demonstration videos on loop, then head up around several different sections showing people working on individual parts of the overall project. You get to see programming testers writing and editing code, and scientists checking the resilience of different materials. You find individual people working on individual movements, such as paw expressions, and groups of people testing how different things synch up when put together on a base frame. Basically, you see every step from start to finish, then head to the company's favourite two rooms. The first is a live demonstration area with a couple of different Familiars ready to help move the original video from imagination to reality for prospective buyers. After that comes the consultation and sales room. It's all very impressive. But it misses a big part of the process.

When I was working on Jonah Burrell's case, I often had to meet him in a factory in the industrial section of the city. You see, these offices do *real* work. Everything that happens here is important. The factory, though, is where mass production takes place, where the final assembly and testing routines are run, and where *your* Familiar is birthed. Personally, I found it all very interesting, but Mr. Burrell was insistent that he couldn't open it up to the public. Yes, there was a degree of danger and disruption to take into account, but he was certain it could be factored in and dealt with. No, image was his main concern. Of the six smaller companies that became FE Ltd, he was convinced four failed because they did not present themselves in a manner consistent with modern sensibilities. He understood that factories such as this were integral if a product like a Familiar was to be made, but his data showed the two companies that did not publicise their backroom grunt work came the closest to succeeding.

So, when he envisioned the Familiar Project, he bought up the companies and set about building a very specific image. This was the face of the modern pet, built by a modern company, and marketed to modern people. There was simply no room for a vintage-looking factory in all of that, because it was too messy, and didn't fit in with the smaller-and-simpler-is-better mentality we're fed in terms of how businesses carry out their work.

I *am* happy to be in the main offices today, though. Well-lit, warm, and not unwelcoming. That's what I need right now.

The receptionist from the phone, Brenda, greets me when I arrive at the third-floor reception desk, and ushers me into a room to await my appointment. Within two minutes, the door at the back of the room opens and a woman peers in, scanning the room until she comes to me. "Cassandra Tam?"

I nod and rise to my feet. "And you must be Mrs. Faraday."

The woman rolls her eyes behind her thick-rimmed glasses and proceeds to untie and retie her scruffy ponytail. "Doctor Faraday, technically. Brenda never remembers that. Shall we?" She nods over her shoulder.

I follow her inside to a small office and take the seat offered at the front of the single desk at the back of the room. "It's like a dentist's waiting room back there."

Faraday shrugs. "It's less like a dentist's place in here, though it took some doing. My first role here was working on teeth, so they made the waiting room look that way as a joke. I do a lot more now, but I kept the same office area, and figured it wasn't important." She flicks her head towards a side door and yawns but keeps her eyes on a small wad of papers she's started rifling through. "The *fun* stuff's in there. Now, what can I do for *you*?"

I ignore the doesn't-want-to-be-here attitude Doctor Faraday is giving off and say, "I had a few concerns about my Familiar Unit, Bert."

"Yes," she cuts in. "Beaked gargoyle. Cute little thing, really. Nothing turned up on his last maintenance trip, and there were no signs of potential degradation, so I assume it's not a physical issue?"

"No. And I'm not even certain what's happening is an issue, exactly. Or not yet, anyway. You see, he's developed some quirks, at least one of which *could* be problematic."

"Okay, so let's hear it. What exactly has he been up to?"

"Well, a lot of it's kinda personality based. He's started picking up new subtle movements, like tapping his claws on the table and narrowing his eyes at me. He's picked up a few more sounds too."

Faraday rests her elbows on the table, crosses her hands, and lowers her chin to the newly made dorsum bridge. She sniffs, wrinkling her nose a little, and replies, "I see. And I assume these behaviours are not the main issue?"

I shake my head. "No, that would be the disobedience."

"Okay. Disobedience in what way?"

"I'm sorry, but do you know what I do for a living?"

"Do you know what *I* do for a living?"

"Uh, not really."

"That's because I didn't tell you. Did you tell me what you did?"

*Charming*, I tell myself, and let out a sigh. "I'm a Private Investigator."

"A detective for hire, then. That would explain Bert's programming, I suppose. Is it when you have him out on a work case that he disobeys you?"

"Yes."

"Can you give me an example?"

"About a month ago, I was working on a case that involved an illegal dogfight. Bert came with me for support and, during my investigation, several stolen dogs were let loose into a room we were both in. I ended up being confronted by one of the dogs—"

"A large dog? Being aggressive?" she interrupts.

"Yeah. I can't remember the breed, but it was definitely being aggressive. Actually, it was scared more than anything. Anyway, I was trying to calm the dog down, and Bert got in between us. I told him to stand down, but he refused."

Faraday sighs and asks, "And does this sort of behaviour happen often?"

"No. In fact, after the police turned up, he *did* back down when told. That was a different dog, though."

"And less aggressive than the first, I bet," Faraday replies. She removes her glasses and gives her eyes a rub, before continuing, "I think I can explain this. Let's start with the new personality-based stuff, as you called it. Putting aside any arguments about robot ethics and the study of AIs in terms of whether or not they can be classed living beings, Bert is on a base level a computer, correct?"

I nod.

"And when you have a computer, the Operating System sometimes downloads updates to improve performance and add new features. While Familiar Units are certainly complex in terms of the more—*subtle* touches, you could certainly view the combined programming as an OS."

I note the pride in Faraday's voice when she says "subtle." I guess she works on the micro-movements. "So, you're saying the new stuff is just wireless updates?"

"To the personality engine, yes. What Bert receives and utilises depends on his own individual parameters, and he'd still *learn* in the sense that any movements or actions causing major upset would likely not be repeated in terms of his general behaviour. Is he destructive at all?"

"Sometimes. I tell him off, but he still *does stuff* if he gets bored."

"Familiars carry out complex scans of living beings. If he detected even a small hint of amusement in your voice when you've told him off, or he got a sense that something he's done has helped ease a burden or concern, the behaviour will be logged as acceptable. In short, he probably knows you about as well as, if not better, than you know yourself. Either that or your discipline skills are lacking."

*Grin and bear it, Cassie.* "Okay, that's good to know. What about the example with the dog?"

"There are two classes of Familiar; Family and Protector. What we have discussed applies primarily to the Family Class. The idea is to create something that reacts much as a flesh-and-blood pet would, albeit with a slight sense of manifested anthropomorphism. Protector Class Units, on the other hand, are built with the primary purpose of, as the name would suggest, protection. They carry out similar scans of living beings but focus on things like aggression and malicious intent. The example you gave means he detected something in the large dog that indicated him backing down would end negatively for you."

*That makes sense. Fish, the dog I was trying to find, clearly leaned more towards scared than ready to attack, so Bert obeyed me when I told him to stand down. He did the same when Charlie pulled the gun on me in her cellar because he knew her, and probably picked up on her lowered aggression when she heard my voice.*

Faraday clicks her tongue a few times and asks, "Do you know how many Familiar Units currently exist with hybrid programming such as Bert's?"

"No."

"To a degree, it exists in most dog-styled Units. Dogs traditionally guard properties, even if they primarily function as a playmate and companion for humans. In these cases, it is only a very small part of their inbuilt personality, however. With Bert, the Family and Protector Classes balance fairly evenly—at your own behest, I may add. There are a few in existence with a version of this style of programming that reside within the third floor of this office. We test them regularly for potential issues and *developments*. Out in the real world, however, Bert is one of only three."

"Why so few?"

"In part, it's because very few people require them. I can certainly understand the need given your line of work, but you must be aware how few people would be able to afford a Familiar Unit on a PI's wage. No, those who would likely benefit from such a setup are rarely in a position to make it a reality. On top of that, the hybrid programming means the Units appear to test boundaries and try new things more often than single class Units. Running things through two different types of programming means they learn more efficiently too, however, and the in-house testing indicates they can often appear more human in nature."

"Which would make most people feel like they're more alive, eh? Sounds like a marketing dream, to me."

"I tell you this only because Mr. Burrell insisted that, should the issues you wished to raise be what he expected them to be, then explaining the situation would be more likely to placate your concerns. We cannot release such things to the general public because there are quite literally a ton of issues we would face, both in terms of potential public reactions, and also relating to breaches of several interlinked contracts. As it is, you were in a position where Mr. Burrell felt you would provide a suitable environment for live testing of the hybrid system."

"And he didn't explain that to me because...?"

"For one, you asked for the programming off your own back, and without prompting. For two, I understand he *did* mention it to a small degree."

I think back to the day I met with Jonah Burrell to discuss my requirements. What did he say? *It is quite rare for someone to request a pure hybrid like this. We don't release too many at all, so in some respects, this will be a learning experience for both of us.*

I smirk and shake my head. "Yeah, he did. Not in detail, but he did mention it."

"I trust you won't be causing any trouble for FE Ltd in relation to this matter?"

I shrug. "No need, is there? You're testing things for safety, and it's not like I have enough information to kick up a stink, even if I thought there was something major going on here."

Faraday nods and intentionally lets me hear the clicking of gears somewhere inside her head. She smiles and adds, "If the *issues* increase significantly in frequency, please do come back to us. Otherwise, you can trust that not only is Bert acting in your best interests, but that you are legally covered should there be a mishap."

"Good to know," I reply, and get to my feet. "I'll show myself out."

Faraday simply watches me leave. I make sure to thank Brenda on the desk too. The question is, how many people in there know? Could Brenda be a bit ditzy, or does she simply refuse to use Faraday's title due to what she is? On top of that, is Faraday one of the in-house test subjects or one of the other two like Bert, out there in the real world? I suspect I'll never know. "I still would have preferred to *know* I was assisting with a test, though," I grumble to myself.


WITH BERT STILL on charge, I decide to spend some time skim reading different parts of the police files Devereaux sent over. The focus for me is to familiarise myself with anything that will (a) make it easier to entice the attacker into trying their luck with me again, and (b) ensure my safety if the PD screw up. Step one is to have the locations of the attacks marked on a map for myself. Yes, there's already a nice big one of those at the station, but I've forgotten what it all looked like already.

By the time I've finished putting the thing together, I'm a little disappointed. I'd hoped that, given the vampire façade, there'd be some sort of easily identifiable cult-like patterning to the layout. Cliché, I know, but it's amazing how many criminals fall into the trap of doing exactly what fiction says. "I guess they all fit inside a pentagram. If I draw it big enough to cover half of Utah State."

Two of the named victims, Jack Stan and Pauline Mensche, I recognise. Both are well-known professional thieves working for the Four Kings of Utah, the group that controls the criminal underworld. Jack works solely for Saul Solomon, and Pauline for Brett Stantz. The other kings, Gory Gutierrez and Kerry White, have their own thieves on call. The problem is, all four kings are in actuality the same person: Allen Fuerza. While I know my comrade-in-arms for this case, Donal O'Brien, is well aware of this fact, I have no idea whether these two are. The police at large definitely aren't, and I can't imagine they had an easy ride getting statements from them. All that means is, just like the file says, they were recovered from the scene, completely unconscious.

None of the other victims have criminal records, or at least nothing worth mentioning in the file, so that removes the likelihood of this being aimed at either the Kings or Fuerza. It shouldn't, but that makes me smile, somehow. "Can't say I'm disappointed about not having to jump down *that* rabbit hole again."

My own file is a little scant, having not yet been updated with my statement. The important thing to note is the PD *did* try to trace the anonymous caller, but they'd had no luck. That could mean the person happened to be using a burner, or they had a high-end security system on their cell to mask their identity. Or it could have been a public phone conveniently angled so as to avoid being caught on security cameras. Regardless of the reason, it does mean that one's a dead end. "No reward for my Good Samaritan, then."

The other fifteen victims who aren't me vary as much as humanly possible. We're covering a wide spectrum of ages, a mix of genders and race, and—according to Devereaux's notes—the full run of social classes too. I frown. "Computer, open server six, primary folder case files, subfolder Orlok, subfolder personal notes. Open file notes and activate dictation at end of current text."

"Dictation activated, please confirm text."

"That the attacker hasn't focused on one clear group fits with Hoove's assertion that these attacks are opportunistic. At the same time, the variety of people who have been attacked is large enough that I'm not sure it *can* be classed as purely random. Yes, the victims were probably picked at random for the most part, but it's possible the attacker had at least some criteria each time. This could be an intentional attempt at sampling a mixed group. Without knowing what has already been tested by the PD, though, I can't be certain if I'm covering old ground here. End dictation and save."

"File saved."

I drum my fingers on the desk. I should probably bring it up with the team as soon as possible. "Computer, set reminder for tomorrow. Reminder text to read as follows. Check opportunistic with criteria theory with team and find out what commonality tests have been carried out."

"Text saved. Please confirm time of reminder and mode of delivery."

"Mode of delivery, audio readout. Time...set tracking mode target, Cassandra Tam, and issue reminder if target tries to leave apartment without confirming the reminder can be cancelled."

"Settings saved."

Next, I run through the cases again, checking them in order of attack. The locations jump about a lot, but there's no discernible pattern to them in that regard. There is also very little variance in the nature of these attacks. Some victims seem to take longer to subdue than others, but that may not count for much. Not only does it tie up with what Devereaux and Hanson already confirmed about the inconsistencies of the presumed tech being used, but it also runs into the territory of some victims trying to talk up their levels of toughness. That probably seems a little cynical. Truthfully, though, I've encountered far too many people with a craving for overselling themselves to not at least consider it in most cases. Especially when the victims in this case come out with quotes like, 'I knew they was tough, 'cause I clonked 'em but good, and it didn't do nothing.'"

Bad English aside, all that statement really confirms is the victim views *himself* as tough. I'm not naive enough to believe how overwhelmed I was means *no one* would be able to throw a punch at this person, but I'm also not naive enough to take every statement at face value.

I sigh, manually shut the tablet down, and move it to the shelving unit nearest to my bedroom door. My phone often ends up there too, as it puts it within range of the wireless charger I picked up last week. It's not near powerful enough to charge Bert, as I don't really want to give him an excuse to spend too long investigating the thing, but it can handle a couple of smaller devices at once, as long as they're within a few metres of it. There are much better models out there, of course, but they all come with rather ludicrous price tags at the moment.

Now, to figure out what I can and can't tell Lori about the case...

LORI ARRIVES AT ten past eight which I take to be a minor miracle. Work for both of us has been in a state of flux recently. Gone are the days of one week of solid work, one week of little to do, and here to stay—for now at least—are the days of rapid-fire peaks and troughs. Although we're getting more time together again, it's rare for us to manage to meet up on time. Ten minutes late is actually a new record for us this past fortnight.

"So, come on," Lori says, and gives me a quick, but tender kiss. "Spill. What happened last night?"

I laugh nervously and make a beeline for the kitchen. "Funny story. Tea or coffee?" I glance over my shoulder and see Lori smiling, her free hand held up with the thumb and forefinger making a "C" shape. That means coffee, 'cause we're cute like that. "So, remember how you told me not to get mugged?"

Lori laughs out loud and moves over to the couch, placing a pleasantly large box of doughnuts on the small table in front of her. "Very good."

I remain silent and continue working on the drinks.

After a moment, Lori says, "Wait... You're being serious?"

"Afraid so," I reply, scooping up the mugs and making the short walk over to sit next to her. "Typical me, eh?"

Lori's eyes twinkle with a sincere concern then, and she gives me a thorough look up and down. "Are you okay?"

"Yes. No. Maybe. I don't know." I shrug and place the mugs down on the table next to the unopened box. "It was...a surprise more than anything."

"It must have been pretty nasty to rattle you like this, though?"

"Yeah. That's one way to put it."

Lori takes my hand and I instinctively grip it. "So, tell me what happened."

I smile and let out a sigh. "You know, I've spent the last hour trying to figure what I *can* tell you? I ended up having to call Captain Hoover over at the station to clarify my position in that regard."

"Okay, now I'm worried."

"Honestly? So am I. Okay, here's what I'm allowed to talk about. I was walking home, heading down Main Street. I guessed you'd mentioned the mugging thing because there's been a few on the news sites lately." Lori nods to confirm I was right, and I continue, "I figured a well-lit area would be safer than my normal route. Anyway, I'd stopped to look at one of the EU25s, and I heard someone calling for help in an alley a few feet away. It was a woman. She'd been attacked. Or that's what she said, anyway. I was already halfway down the alley by the time I'd realised there wasn't a woman there at all."

I pause to take a drink, and Lori asks, "Did they take much?"

I shake my head and swallow the molten caffeine. "One mugger, and they didn't end up taking anything. Which is how I've ended up in the mess I have."

"How do you mean?"

"Not all of the recent muggings are by the same people, but a few of them are clearly linked, my own included. I'm not allowed to say how exactly, not yet, but the ones like mine aren't regular muggings. The problem is because this person didn't get what they wanted, there's a possibility they'll try again. That's what the police are banking on."

Lori blinks in disbelief and turns to her coffee, a thoughtful expression drifting over her face. She gently shakes the drink back and forth, creating a mini whirlpool in her mug. Finally, she states, "They want to use you to trap this person."

"I'm even less happy about it than you are," I grumble, and mean every word of it.

"Do you at least get some backup on this?"

"There's a small team involved, three I know well enough to trust, and one who I don't know, but who I'm pretty certain is more than competent at his job. He heads the PD's TS Unit."

Lori tilts her head towards the ceiling, trying to remember something, then asks, "Donal O'Brien?"

"That's him," I reply, slowly.

"I was there when he was interviewed about a case a month or so back. It was a raid on an arms trader. He's efficient, definitely. I mean, he had a few others with him, but my understanding is he took down a couple of really dangerous guys on his own. He said it was a team thing, of course, but you don't get to lead a unit without knowing what you're doing, right?"

"That sounds encouraging."

Lori nods. "You said *person*. That means there was only one attacker. If you've got Donal O'Brien playing bodyguard, then unless they're *really* scary, you should be fine. Who else is involved?"

"Captain Hoover, Lieutenant Hanson, and Corporal Devereaux."

Lori lets out a sigh of relief. I've mentioned all three before, and always in a positive manner, so that will have helped. In a way, it makes it easier to keep the other details in. If she was scared when I was up against a regular thief, she'd be terrified if she knew I was up against a vampire. "If I tell you to stay safe, will you actually do it this time?"

"No promises," I say, throwing in a cheeky grin and an unnecessary wink.

Lori giggles and makes a grab for the doughnut box. "Well, I can't fault your honesty. Still, that means I get first pick."

The box, as it turns out, is packed tight with six jelly-filled doughnuts I can only describe as larger-than-your-average-doughy-treat. My eyes flick over the blueberry filled mass in the far corner, and I watch as Lori lets her own hand hover over it for a few seconds, before heading straight for the apple doughnut next to it. She teases, but she knows my favourites. Without asking, Lori turns the box so that my target is closer to me, and says, "I think someone deserves a treat after such a traumatic experience."

"No arguments from me," I reply and snatch up my prize.

"I love how much of a pig you are with doughnuts, you know that?"

"First lesson in police academy," I mumble through an overestimated mouthful and end up having to wipe my chin with my finger. "So, what about you? Was the open house more interesting than my play date with New Hopeland's finest?"

"Depends on your views, I guess. You aren't the only one taking an interest in the EU25s, though."

"No?"

"A couple of people are claiming they contain non-advertised tech designed to keep track of citizens. They tied it all into the recent concerns about data monitoring and the alleged hidden security cameras."

"I thought they were proven to be disused, older systems?"

"They were, but you know how the conspiracy theory crowd can be. For every plausible idea, there's ten cases of denying clear evidence that goes against their views. Took up a fair bit of time too."

"And how did the city reps deal with it?"

"Well enough that I'm guessing they expected it. Most of the day was what you expect from these things; individual people with individual problems who already have a proper channel to report through, and no hope of any answer in a public forum. The talk about tax reforms and reallocation of monetary resources sounded interesting enough, but it was littered with enough jargon and governmental-speak to go over my head a lot of the time. The basic message was that local taxes will remain broadly similar for most, but there will be a shift in what projects get the lion's share of the takings."

"Some things never change," I say, and grab a raspberry-filled goody. Lori takes the apricot.

THE MORNING COMES peacefully.

I blink my eyes open and push myself closer to Lori. I'm gentle enough not to wake her but allow myself to feel the warmth of her body against mine as I wrap an arm over her bare stomach. It was a warm night, so we forewent sleepwear. It's not like we planned anything, so Lori would have been stuck with my stuff anyway, which in some cases would have hung so loosely they would have been far from flattering. Lying next to me, Lori lets out a quiet snore, and I can't help but smile. I doubt she'd see it the same way if I mentioned it, but I think it's cute. There's a contentedness to it that I really like.

With my morning vision now finally clearing, I gently press my forehead to the back of Lori's, resting it against one of her plugs. I take in a deep breath and the smell of rubber and metal fills my nose. It's a strange thing to like given my confused feelings about the Tech Shifting community in general, but it's something so intertwined with Lori herself that it's easy to take it for what it is. It's part of her natural scent, and something I recognise with ease now. There's more to it, of course. The smell of her usual shampoo, the ageing leather on her jacket, the slight sweat she builds up during certain *activities;* all the normal stuff people don't always realise they recognise in someone.

But *I* notice it. I don't know whether it's my habit of analysing every little thing, or that I'm just happy. I can't even remember now if I had the same experience with Charlie. If I did, I don't think I ever fully acknowledged it. Lori's different, though, in more ways than one. She doesn't mind that I sometimes don't need a nudge so much as a fully-fledged shove to get over myself. And she understands that we both get it wrong sometimes. This all feels new to me, and as stupid as it sounds, part of me hopes it feels the same to her.

Lori lets out a low murmur and rolls onto her back, blinking her eyes open to meet mine. She returns my smile and lifts her head to give me a quick kiss before stretching her legs and saying, "Morning."

"Morning. Coffee?"

"You read my mind." She yawns. "Sorry. *Someone* kept me up all night."

"Cheeky," I reply, playfully flicking her nose. "Need I remind you that *you're* the one who convinced me to stop being so nervous?"

"I've created a monster," she teases, piling on the melodrama as she rises to a sitting position and starts stretching her arms behind her head.

Do I take a moment to watch the morning light creep over her? Yes. Yes, I do. But hey, she's doing the same to me while I fumble for a dressing gown, so it's only fair. "Do you fancy some breakfast?"

"Coffee's fine. I'll need to get home and change before work anyway, so I probably shouldn't stay too long."

"Fair enough. We never did get to the last two doughnuts, though, so you could always take one of those for a sugar boost. You know, providing you can put it in your mouth the right way this time."

"Sure. I'll save it for the car, just in case. Sadly, I don't have the time to spill jelly over myself and set you off again."

I head to the kitchen, my cheeks already reddening behind a smile full of memories. The rest of the morning is just as jovial. We joke about introducing Ink to Bert and talk a little about it in seriousness too. It's gotta happen eventually, but with him acting up, I'm not sure we should risk it yet. Then, when all is said and done, Lori heads home and I hit the shower.

I needed last night. And this morning. It'd be easy to dwell on the fact that, had I accepted Lori's lift home, I wouldn't have woken in a police cell yesterday. But I won't do that. The past cannot be changed, and I choose to stand by my decisions, even when they've led me into less than favourable situations. The coming days will be difficult, but really, I'm just doing what I've always done. What I've always wanted to do. I'm trying to make sure the bad guys don't win.

# Chapter Three

WHEN I ARRIVE at the station, the day is already in full swing. Cops are busy making calls, abusing holographic keyboards with overly aggressive finger jabs, and rifling through hard copy printouts from various cases. The workload is heavy. I've heard rumours of stations in other areas giving their staff fake jobs to do when they're in the public's line of sight, with the idea being that it would help eliminate the persistent stereotype of lazy cops doing nothing all day on the taxpayer's dime. Honestly, though, I fully expect the work going on here to be legit. Even putting aside the sheer amount of crime that goes down in New Hopeland, the PD's visible leadership isn't fond of the smoke and mirrors routine unless it becomes an absolute necessity.

Speaking of which, I spot Hoove patrolling the various desks, chatting with his staff, and wait for a chance to catch his eye. When he looks up long enough to spot me, he nods towards the hallway to the war room. I start making my way through the mass of busy people, and someone I vaguely recall speaking to once or twice stands up to stop me. Before he can say anything, Hoove yells over, "Let her through, jackass," and he does so with a grunt.

I'm about halfway down the hallway when he jogs up behind me. "I never knew you were so agile," I say.

He snorts. "Gotta keep up with the youngsters. You gonna be okay with all this?"

I shrug. "I've got to be, haven't I?"

"Only as far you need to be to get through it. I know I didn't give you much choice in how involved you are, and believe me, I'd love to be more flexible, but that doesn't mean you have to suffer in silence. If things get tough, or if you feel like anyone is stepping out of line, talk to me."

"And by anyone, you mean Donal O'Brien, right?"

"I mean *anyone*, but yeah. He's a good cop, and he'll be invaluable on this, but he's as capable of being a dick as everyone else. That he was so willing to work with you is out of character too. No offence."

*It's not surprising*, I tell myself. *Fuerza and Sunglasses work fast.* Out loud, I reply, "Good to know. And thanks, Hoove."

"Don't mention it," he says and pushes the door to the war room open.

Inside, Corporal Devereaux is busy adding two new marks to the incident map. He stops when he hears the door shut and glances over at us, giving a vague acknowledgement of, "Captain. Cassie," before starting to rifle through some papers.

"We all good to go?" Hoove asks.

"Sure are." Devereaux smiles. "Donal's getting suited up as we speak."

"We got a lead?" I ask.

Devereaux shakes his head. "Some new victims, one for a follow-up interview, one for an initial interview, but otherwise no. We made some modifications to Donal's TS gear that *should* work to counter the light show. Well, providing we're right about the way it works, eh?"

I nod. "So it's testing time."

"That's the idea," Hoove replies. "Let's head down there."

We leave the room and head to the ramp to the basement levels of the station, skipping over the weapon storage floor and heading straight for the TS Unit floor. When we get down there, I follow quietly behind my case comrades until we reach an open room with a padded floor that is clearly set up to act as a gym. From the claw marks on the floor and the walls, the TS Unit obviously make good use of it. Hanson is already waiting for us, restlessly swinging two torch-like devices around in a complex arc pattern. *She's not doing the footwork, but I recognise the movements. It's not a standard police technique, though. I'll have to ask her about it later.*

"Stop mucking around with the equipment," Hoove grunts, and Hanson stops in her tracks.

"Sorry. Got bored," she replies, shooting us a cheeky wink.

"You got bored?" Hoove sighs. "And if you'd broken the damn things, swinging them about like majorette batons, then what would you say?"

Hanson shrugs. "Whoops?"

The put-upon police captain rubs the bridge of his nose and grumbles, "You're lucky you're so damn good at your job." He looks over to an open door at the back of the room and yells, "Are you ready yet, O'Brien?"

"Just about," an artificially amplified voice booms. Moments later, the loud *clack-clack* of heavy, metal claws rings out from the shadows, and Donal O'Brien joins us on the mats.

In his full gear, the Irishman adds a further half a foot, give or take, to his frame. He must have been about six five already, so the height alone goes a long way to creating a truly imposing image. Even without that, he'd strike fear into anyone, no matter whether they knew about the Murder

Files or not. Donal's TS form is that of an ash grey anthropomorphic wolf, and unlike the rounded tips of the publicly available TS gear, his enforcement-modded suit has claws that could tear more than the pads in this room. Even the teeth in his metallic snout appear longer and sharper than those on Lori's Ink. "Let's get started," he says, then shouts, "Lights off."

They go off on command, leaving only the light seeping in from the hallway behind us, and Hanson says, "We'll use the Dazzler first." She steps forward onto the mat and raises one hand. A quiet *click* sounds, and all of a sudden, the torch in her hand is emitting a ridiculously bright green light at Donal O'Brien's metal-covered chin. She lifts her hand and readjusts her aim, shining it straight at the Tech Shifter's eyes.

Donal O'Brien doesn't move.

"Anything?" Devereaux asks.

"Nothing," Donal replies. Hanson clicks another switch and the light starts to pulsate at different rates. "Still nothing. Try the Incapacitator."

Hanson clicks the torch off and brings up another, this time landing her first shot straight in the eyes. After a few seconds, Donal says, "Still nothing. You get the homebrew finished?"

"You know I did," Hanson replies, a smile reaching her voice. The torch flickers off, and she pulls something out of the back of her pants. Another flashing light hits Donal's face, and he remains unflinching.

"Okay, that'll do. Lights on."

The lights come back up, and Hanson turns to face us. "First one was a military grade Dazzler. Second one was a police issue model. The third is something you can put together using tech you can pick up in stores. Looking good, ain't it?"

"So, how did you counter it?" I ask.

"Eye guard," Donal replies. "You won't see it from over there 'cause it's clear, but it has a covering made from vanadium doped zinc telluride. It's an old technique to deal with Dazzler weapons, but it still works. It'll take a day or two to get some non-TS equivalents ready for ya all, though."

"That's fine," Hoove says with a smile.

"Not to put a dampener on it all, but how do you know for sure they're working?" I ask. "The weapons are inconsistent, right?"

Donal tilts a far too threatening muzzle towards me and says, "I had them tested on me when we came up with the theory. Well, not the homebrew one, but the other two. Believe me when I say they work fine on me."

I nod. "Fair enough."

"Okay," Hoove interjects. "Next task is to get ready for today's calls. Devereaux, Hanson, make sure you've got the updated files and head to victim twenty. Caz, I'm gonna need to get you tooled up before you and Donal can head out to number nineteen."

"Tooled up? How do you mean?"

"WHAT ARE YOU carrying these days?" Hoove asks once we're back on the weapons storage floor.

"Glock Vintage."

"The 23 model?" he asks, and I nod. He rolls his eyes and unholsters his own gun, holds it out to me and says, "Trust you to go retro. You seen one of these before?"

I take the handgun and turn it over in my hands. "Looks like a HK45."

"Mk 33. Same as most modern upgrades; fingerprint recognition, multiple tip compatibility, more accurate sighting. These ones are running Jolt."

"The auto correction pack? I didn't think it was out of testing yet."

"It isn't. We may not be at the forefront as a city anymore, but we still get to try out the new shit." Hoove takes the gun back from me and taps a small sheet of metal, barely raised above the top of the barrel. "This thing's loaded with a camera and a heart-rate scanner at the front. Point it at a perp until the back end goes green, and it'll track them. If your aim's gonna be off, it pushes your hand in the right direction to correct it."

"So I hear. How does it work?"

"You get a lightweight palm pad on your non-trigger hand, and it uses magnets to force you in the right direction."

We stop outside the door to the war room and I frown. "How accurate is it, though? Like, if you're going for a precision kill, what if it thinks you'll potentially miss and readjusts to something non-lethal?"

"You'll get to see that soon enough."

"How do you mean?"

"You're licenced to carry the Glock, so you can keep that on you if you like. These are the standard now, so all the while you're working with us, you'll need to be signed off on one of them."

*Change? Again? We hate that! Abort!*

I silently shoo away my brain's reaction to the sheer amount of change I've had in my life recently. Some of it hasn't been bad, but my standing with Allen Fuerza and whatever he's up to isn't as welcome. Knowing he's been secretly running most of Utah's criminal underworld for years now isn't exactly comforting, even if his reasoning for doing so makes sense. That he could just decide to have me killed any time he wants doesn't help.

Hoove hands me a thin square of leather with straps hanging off the shaven corners and shows me how to attach it to my hand. Next, he plugs a fresh HK45 Mk 33 into the nearby computer terminal using a cable similar to the one that came with my phone when it was new. I wrap my fingers around the grip on the gun's frame and wait until the machine confirms I'm registered for use. Next, he leads me through a side door to a small shooting range and, after rummaging through a drawer, hands me a clip of what I'm assuming are blanks. While I load them into the gun, he taps a couple of buttons on the keypad on the wall and a mannequin rises in the background.

"Okay, quick tutorial. The mannequin is equipped with a simulated pulse. Point the gun at it and hold your aim... There, see the thin green strip at the back of the raised panel? That means you have a lock. Now, fire a couple of rounds. Put one in the shoulder, and one in the chest."

I widen my stance and readjust my aim, carefully picking my spot. In a real-life situation, I'd move quicker. Necessity and muscle memory are useful companions when you're in a situation where you need to start wheeling out gun play. Here in a controlled environment, and under the watchful eye of the person who constitutes my commanding officer for the duration of the case, I'm happy to take my time. Well, not happy really. Comfortable with the usefulness of it. As such, when I *do* squeeze the trigger, I'm certain it's helping instil the right sort of muscle memory in me.

"Both spot on," Hoove says. "Now, I want you to aim for the shoulder again, but let your hand drift to the side and down a bit."

"To the arm?"

"No. Try to miss, but not by much."

I do as I'm told and, just as I start to pull on the trigger, I feel a jolt in the palm pad and my aim is forced almost violently back into place. A check of the mannequin shows that I hit a little above where I hit it the first time. "*Diu.*"

Hoove gives his moustache a thoughtful scratch and says, "It has limits. Try aiming all the way over there."

I follow the direction of his finger to the far corner of the range and do as he said. Again, when I try to pull the trigger, the palm pad springs to life. This time, my arm is yanked back towards the mannequin at a terrifying speed, almost causing me to drop the weapon. "Damn thing nearly dislocated my shoulder," I growl through gritted teeth.

"You missed too. It'll try to fix your aim, but it's not a miracle solution by any means. Now, here's a question for you. When you aimed at the chest, were you going for a kill?"

"No, not intentionally. Did I catch a kill spot?"

"No, you didn't. Okay. In that case, try for the head."

I give my shoulder a few quick rotations to loosen it up again and do as I'm told. I line up the barrel, steady myself, and squeeze the trigger. Again, the palm pad forces my aim to change, dragging it down to the shoulder. "What the...?"

"There's the kicker with the Jolt system, at least how it is. The standard setting is non-lethal. In our experience thus far, it's spot-on with being able to tell if you'll hit the target most of the time, and I'm talking in the high nineties there. If it can tell you're going for a kill, though, it'll *correct* your aim to the nearest non-lethal point."

"So how *do* you carry out a precision kill? You can't tell me police departments are honestly going to be expected to work without that as a potential."

"Of course not. The first models had an audio recognition thing built in. You had to say 'Kill Box' out loud to the gun to get it to loosen up. You can imagine how well that worked when you had to go into noisy areas. I tell ya, if we hadn't been carrying the pre-Jolt models too, there would have been a few less cops on the streets after that debacle. The one you're holding is working with an improved system. Take aim again. Now, the hand you've got on the grip? Tap your little finger on the grip twice, and fire."

I do so, and this time, my bullet flies true, impacting in the mannequin's forehead, a little off where I wanted, but not so much as to make a difference to the end result.

"I don't like it," I say, honestly. "I don't have to use guns often, but when I do, I'm used to just aiming and firing. This adds an extra step to the process. What if someone forgets to do the tap in a life and death situation?"

"My advice is *don't*. What really sucks is it won't let you fire without a lock unless you double tap too, but with your ring finger. We're strongly recommending that feature is removed. Like I said, keep your Glock with you if you're more comfortable knowing it's there, but you're gonna have to at least try with this, or you'll be giving the higher-ups more ammo. They're only partially sold on your involvement as it is. Oh, and the kill setting is time-limited once activated. Ten seconds, unlimited shots in that time, or as many as you can get out of the clip anyway."

"Great."

"Sorry, Caz, it is what it is. The final release should have the targeting as optional, but we're stuck with this at the moment. Look at it like this, though. With the way the LV works, it should be useful in making sure we can actually hit the thing, even if the light show solution isn't working. Anyway, we can't hide down here all day. Grab yourself a couple of live clips from the drawer over there and meet up with Donal out back. He'll fill you in on the victim."

"Sure, sure," I say, walking to the drawer. "And LV? Is that what we're calling the perp now?"

"Yup. It stands for Light-Vamp. Came up with it last night. Cute, ain't it?"

I roll my eyes but can't keep a small smile from forming on my lips. "Yeah. Real cute."


I BUNDLE INTO the back of a police van. It's not the type the PD normally uses to transport criminals, but rather one of the ones they use to transport personnel. I'd say it was overkill to take two people to a routine interview, but looking at Donal O'Brien slightly hunched up opposite me, I can understand why it's needed. There's no way he's fitting in a regular car, not fully suited.

"Don't worry, it's soundproofed," he says when he spots me glancing over towards the wall leading to the driver. "Unless the green light is on above the hatch, nobody's listening, so it's fine to talk about the case."

I rest back against the wall of the van and sigh. "You've given away that something's up."

"How do ya mean?"

"Captain Hoover said it was odd you were so willing to work with me. I don't suppose he knows who else you work for, does he?"

"Nah. And it's not like I never play nice, so it won't be as big a deal as you're making out. If he mentions it, I'll just point out the obvious."

"That if me being bait is so important, it makes sense for you to be working with me?"

"Exactly."

"Okay, so what do I need to know about the victim? This is a follow-up meeting, so that means the brunt of the statement has already been taken, right?"

Donal stretches his metal-covered arms and crosses his claws behind his masked face. "Name's Joe Farrah. Mid-forties, licenced gun shop owner, got attacked in the early part of yesterday evening, right inside his store. Whoever this person is, they're learning too; cut the power before entering, likely to avoid cameras, alarms, and all that shite."

"Pretty brazen, breaking into somewhere so well-armed by default."

"Aye. No fear, that's for sure. Not yet anyway. Once their fancy little light show ain't working, I'll teach 'em to fear."

I smirk. "Sounds like you're taking this all as a challenge."

"Oh, it *is* a challenge. You mark my words."

"Macho posturing aside, how is this gonna work? I get why you're suited up, but won't that cause panic if you get out into the public? I mean, you're pretty recognisable, eh?"

"I am that." Donal chuckles. "Don't worry, it's all been thought of. There's a wireless mic under your seat. You go in with that on, I'll listen in. Any problems, I come running."

"Is that wise? I'm not dressed like a cop, and I don't have a badge to flash. What's to stop him—justifiably—refusing to speak to me?"

"Ah, he won't do that. It's no accident we got this one, I requested him. Called ahead and let him know *you'd* be speaking to him, and everything."

I groan. "He's King's Guard, isn't he?"

"He is that."

"If he's gonna be fine with talking to me, is that because you told him it was okay, or because he knows I know who Allen Fuerza is?"

"Both." I treat Donal to my best incredulous stare and he laughs, then continues, "Fact is, you figured it out and lived to tell the tale. There ain't many who do that. Castleford? The reason for keeping him alive was obvious to anyone in the know. But you? You're different. There's no way you should still be breathing, yet here you are. It makes you special."

"I didn't survive to get famous," I state flatly.

"And I didn't take my job to work under a criminal, but that's the way the chips fell. Look, this is an easy job. Officially, he'll back up what he was told by Corporal Devereaux in the first interview. Off the record, we may get something useful."

"Thick as thieves, eh?"

"If you like," Donal replies with a shrug.

I sigh. "So, is Devereaux doing most of the interviews?"

"Aye. In part, it's because he's the lowest rank of all of us. Well, us full-timers anyway. He's good at it, though. Has a way about him that puts people at ease. Makes 'em more likely to believe the misdirection."

"Yeah. He's a nice guy."

"Hanson certainly seems to think so."

I narrow my eyes at the hulking mass of metal wolf. "Does she?"

"Looks that way to me. Feel free to prod her about it."

"Why not prod her yourself if you're interested?"

"I like my balls right where they are, thank you very much. Yours are metaphorical. Plus, she likes you better."

I laugh and shake my head. This is a far from ideal situation for me, but it could be worse. I don't dislike Donal so far, and if the case gets a few people off my back, even if I didn't know they were there in the first place, it's no bad thing. I am still curious about one thing. "So, how did

Devereaux get involved with this? It feels way above his pay grade, at least in this place."

"It is. He took the first few calls. When the Captain took the cases from him, he kept himself in the loop, I'm guessing through Hanson, and kinda interjected himself. His theory about the LED Incapacitators pretty much got him in the door after that."

"Huh. Who knew he was so forceful?"

"Depending how this all plays out, this case could make him. Can't say I'd be upset about it, either. He's one of the good guys."

I nod in agreement.


HE MAY HAVE been expecting me, but Joe Farrah clearly isn't one hundred per cent happy about the whole situation. Even if I *am* special, I'm still not really part of this particular circle; I'm more like a hangnail on Fuerza's power play. Regardless, being at his place of work at least seems to keep Joe from getting too worked up.

"Extra locks," he says, tapping a massive chunk of metal on the back door to the building. He grabs a hair tie from his pocket and pulls the remainder of his hair into a ponytail, obviously refusing to let a severely receding hairline stop him from leading the fashion side of the rock star lifestyle. "He ain't getting in here again."

"So, you're certain it was a male?" I ask.

"Damn right I am. Didn't you read the report?"

I shake my head. "I got sent straight over here after I arrived, and all I know at the moment is what Donal told me."

"Ugh. Fine. Short version: before I dropped, I managed to grab hold of him. Tried to twist his arm but didn't have the time before the light got to me. The noise he made was male, though, whatever way you cut it."

"Okay, that's something to work with at least. I don't suppose you got any photos or videos before he cut the power?"

Joe laughs. "Don't you think I woulda said something already if I did?"

"Honestly? No. As far as I know, you're going along with the official story in terms of details. Or what you're saying to the public anyway. Showing off footage of your attacker wouldn't really fit with that, would it?"

Farrah lets out a *tch* and shakes his head. "No, it wouldn't. The answer's still no, though. He clearly did his research, knew what to fiddle with before the attack, and knew when it would just be me here. Sammy out there was long gone by then."

"Sammy," I repeat, thinking back to the young man watching the counter while I speak to Joe. "Didn't his name tag say Alex?"

Joe shrugs. "When he starts doing a good job, I'll bother to remember his name."

I sigh. "I get you weren't expecting to speak with me, but Donal's listening in just fine," I say, pointing to the mic attached to my tie. "We'll make sure the official files show you're playing ball. Off the record, is there anything useful you can give us?"

Joe wrinkles his nose at me and lets out a frustrated grunt. "There isn't anything else. Sometimes, things just happen so damn quickly you aren't prepared for it. This is like that."

WE RECEIVED A call just before I made it back to the truck, so as soon as I'm seated, we start heading back to the station.

"Smile," Donal says, studying the morose mood that's washed over me. "We got some stuff to work with."

"That's what worries me."

"You're not bent outta shape about not being told he identified the attacker as male, are ya? I just wanted to avoid influencing what he said. See if he stuck to his story, yeah?"

"I figured that."

"Then what's the problem?"

"Later," I reply.

To his credit, Donal leaves it alone, and we travel the rest of the way in silence. Once we make it back to the station, we head straight for the war room. Hoove is already there waiting for us and goes to grab some drinks while we wait for Devereaux and Hanson to return. Once we're alone again, I turn to Donal and say, "Okay, one question. How many of the victims have an association with either the Kings or Fuerza that hasn't been mentioned in the official files?"

"Two. Joe was one, you don't need to know the other one. I know where you're heading with this, and you're wrong. This isn't something that's aimed squarely at the Underworld. And in case you were wondering, neither Pauline Mensche or Jack Stan know the truth about the Kings."

I nod.

Captain Hoover returns, with both Hanson and Devereaux in tow. We all settle down and the New Hopeland PD's most decorated moustache asks, "So, what have we got? Hanson?"

Hanson smiles and takes a gulp of something vaguely resembling tea from a plastic cup—no more good stuff now we're getting serious—and says, "Maybe nothing. The victim, Mary Warner, was already out cold and on her way to the surgeon when we got there. She was due for an op already they said, but no one would clarify what it was other than that it wasn't anything suspicious. What *was* interesting was the last X-ray showed a foreign body lodged in her arm. Or fragments of one anyway. Could be nothing, but Doctor Sanderson said he'd make sure he recovers it in case we can get something from it."

"Fingers crossed then," Hoover grumbles, then turns to look at me and Donal. "And you two?"

"He's accepted the official story," Donal says. "No sign of anyone stalking Cassie yet, though."

"Did he give us any more information?"

"No. But he's sticking to the idea of the attacker being male. We made sure not to prompt him on that."

"There might have been *something*," I interject.

"Okay," Hoove replies. "Let's hear it."

"He said the attacker had clearly done his research. He knew how to cut the power, and he knew when Mr. Farrah was alone. I know we're working to the concept of the attacks being opportunistic, and that makes sense given the lack of clear links to tie all the victims together, but I'm not certain it's entirely right."

"Because the victim sample is so varied that there being no one clear link could be symptomatic of intentionally picking a wide group," Hanson says. "Yeah, I thought about that too. The problem is, it's a tough one to prove."

"Agreed," I say. "Think about this, though. If the attacker really did do his research on Joe Farrah, and it wasn't just dumb luck, then we could be looking at something else here. Let's say the victims are picked entirely at random, it could be that's where the opportunistic side of things finishes. Maybe he did his research on all his victims, but only after he'd picked them."

"So you're saying he's only opportunistic until he starts to...I dunno...*hunt*?" Devereaux asks.

I shrug. "Maybe. Or maybe it varies from victim to victim. He could have a focus on some victims in particular, or he could stumble upon ideal circumstances for an attack for others."

Hoover rubs his moustache thoughtfully and says, "There's no harm in doing a check, just in case we've missed something. Anyone else got anything they wanna add?" The room remains silent and he continues, "In that case, you're all dismissed. Head to your desks and start going through the files again to test Caz's theory."

"And what about me?" I ask. "Should I head home, or stick by here?"

"If he *is* planning a second attempt, I doubt it'll happen here. I don't want to leave you completely unguarded, though. How safe will you be at home?"

"I have Bert," I reply.

Hoove thinks about it, then nods. "Fine. But if anything happens, call us in *immediately*."

I MAKE GOOD time and get home pretty quickly. I'm so preoccupied with trying to remember any snippets of case files that may help prove some premeditation it takes me a moment to realise something is very strange: the apartment is silent. When I left this morning, Bert was still an hour away from full charge. While that initially seemed like an excessive charge time, it soon became clear he'd been running updates for half the night, which had drained him quite a bit. Usually, he can detach himself once he's ready to go, but every now and then he gets stuck. Glancing over at the charger in the kitchen, he's neither still plugged in, nor waiting for me to plug him back in.

Slowly, I draw the HK45 Hoove gave me, and wait for the light on the top to signal that it's read my fingerprints and is going to cooperate if I need to fire. Good job I left the leather hand guard on my other hand too; I have no idea if the Jolt system would even let me use the thing without it, at least once the targeting kicks in. Looking around the room, there's no sign of a struggle, which means any intruder was either quickly dispatched, or managed to best my little metal menace with ease. The lack of a *clack-clack* to greet me certainly makes the latter seem possible, which fills me with both sadness and a sense of dread.

Keeping my feet near to the ground, I move as swiftly as I can without making a sound and peer into the open bathroom. The mirror on the wall allows me to get a good look without needing to enter the room. Empty. Next stop is the only other room that isn't open plan: my bedroom. I pull the gun out in front of myself, my finger ready to squeeze the trigger if anyone unexpected gets in my line of sight. I step sideways through the door and...find Bert perched silently on the windowsill, staring out at the building across the road.

At first, I think he's gone into a shutdown, but when I get close, he lets out a "Caw" of greeting. Frowning, I follow his line of sight and let my eyes scan both the apparently suspicious apartment block and the street below. I can't see anything of note. Most of the windows are not yet covered by either curtains or the evening security shutters, so I can see a little way into each room. Not far, sure, but enough to know that no one is visibly watching me back. I holster the gun and give Bert a pat on his head. "Silly little bugger. Just like the sugar, eh?"

It's funny, but seeing that Bert is okay and on guard, even if he's not watching anything in particular, is enough to slow my heart, which had been beating rapidly up until a moment ago. *So, how should I celebrate this momentous victory in paranoia cessation? With a coffee and a browse of police files, of course.*

I give some thought to my own experience with Mr. Vamp but come to the uncomfortable conclusion that it will be impossible to ascertain whether any planning went into the attack without actually questioning him. My own movements are fairly varied, even on days when I'm not working a case. He *could* have followed me around for a few days to try to pick up any behaviours that would give them an in, or to wait patiently for an opening, but there's no evidence to prove *or* disprove that. An attack at home would have been difficult for two reasons. The first is Mr. Mayhem in the bedroom. The second is the simple fact that I'm on the fifteenth floor. No, *I* appear to be a dead end.

Sticking with the link to the Kings, given that Joe Farrah appears to have been a victim of meticulous planning, I follow up on Jack Stan and Pauline Mensche next. Jack was attacked in the parking lot behind the New Hopeland Central Theatre. As I learned when I was working the Kitsune case, the theatre isn't exactly tooled up with the highest quality surveillance equipment. The result of that is we do have a blurry video of someone shrouded in light moving towards someone else presumably off-screen. There's no video of their exit, though. Jack was pretty vague about why he was at the theatre, simply stating he was there for a show, which in fairness to him could be true. That there were no other witnesses makes it unlikely, as unless he was leaving early or arriving late, you'd expect other people to be around. My guess is he was running a job and would have been trying to get in. I could check if I really need to. I don't want to, but I may have to.

Pauline's is a little more straightforward. She crashed her car after the attacker jumped on it. That she was found to be carrying a small bag of Delta-S, a synthetic stimulant designed to be a souped-up weed substitute, gave the PD a reason to check with the Dealers to see if the sale had been carried out that night. It hadn't, so they didn't pursue it. They could have tried following the trail to get a quick arrest on whoever she bought from, but that would have been a lot of work for a minimal return, given the nature of the main investigation. Now, if *I* can find out who she bought from, I may be able to get something out of this.

Lieutenant Hanson was attacked a block from her home. Drawn into an alley in a similar way to me and jumped. Was it just a convenient trick to use, or did whoever's behind this play up on both of us having jobs focused on helping others? There was a nurse in there among the victims, I think...yes, Todd Dalton. He was attacked directly, the same as Jack Stan, though. But again, there's a convenience factor there. A direct move could have been easier in that case.

Looking at the files objectively, the same can be said of all of them. The lack of witnesses indicates the guy is at least careful, but we're so low on detail concerning previous days that there's no real way to tell for sure just how much, if any, planning went into this. Too many follow-up interviews now would also raise suspicions with the victims, so knowing where we'd need to focus things off our own backs would be difficult to figure out. We could work with a small sample, I guess.

"Ugh. Okay, Cassie, take the direct approach. Chase up the Jack Stan and Pauline Mensche stuff first, then look at whether the sample needs broadening."

I relax back into my chair and cross my arms behind my head. My eyes drift over to the door to my bedroom, and in particular, the lack of Bert materialising. I close my eyes and think about possible reasons he'd still be there. "Computer, activate speaker phone and dial Captain Hoover, New Hopeland PD."

"Please wait…"

The phone rings out twice over the apartment speakers, followed by a click and a familiar voice. "Captain Hoover."

"Hoove, it's Caz. Something's bugging me. Mind if I run it by you?"

"Sure," he replies, and I can hear the smile in his voice.

"You said our vampire wasn't likely to attack me at the station, and I think you're right about that. The thing is, seeing as I'm bait, you wouldn't send me out into a situation where an attack could happen without being in control of it."

"Yeah, that's right. That's why I checked whether you'd be okay at home. Having Bert there gives you an edge if anything happens."

"It does. Okay then, question. Why is Bert in my bedroom, staring out of the window at the apartment block across the road from me?" Hoove goes silent and I take a deep breath. "Please tell me your silence is symptomatic of you feeling guilty about stationing a guard without telling me."

"I wish it were. Is there any sign of movement?"

"No. Either Bert is keeping them at bay, or they're just watching. That's assuming it's our man, of course."

"Shit."

"Language, Captain."

"Sorry, would you prefer something stronger? I have a few choice phrases I only pull out for special occasions."

I let out a short, sharp laugh and reply, "Okay, look. *If it's who we're looking for, they don't seem to be making any moves to come up here. According to the files, all the attacks have taken place in secluded, dark areas. If I stick to populated, well-lit areas, I should be fine...*"

"You're planning to go out?" Hoove cuts in.

"I'm gonna have to. One of the victims, Jack Stan, is a professional thief working for Saul Solomon. That indicates the attacker isn't on the Kings of Utah's payroll. If I can get an audience with Mr. Solomon, I can at least find out if the attack took place during a job. That'll add credence to the theory about the attacks being planned, at least in some cases."

"And what makes you think you'd even get an audience with one of the Kings? Last I checked, they weren't exactly social butterflies."

"The car chase that's come back to bite me in the ass? During the case, I learned something. The Underground views me as having more of a foot in the dark side than you guys do. I'm banking on it being enough to get me in the door. After that, I'm safe, at least while I'm there. You'd have to be insane to attack someone during a meeting with the Kings, eh?"

Hoove gives a heavy sigh and replies, "I suppose that's true. But how are you gonna get a meeting set up in the first place?"

"I'll go through Devin Carmichael."

"Caz, when was the last time you got involved with *him*, and it didn't lead to trouble?"

"Trouble is his job. Mine too right now."

"Difference being *we* can control this a little. *No one* holds sway over him."

"It'll be fine."

"I doubt that, somehow."

"How about this then? Give me Donal's number, and I'll let him know roughly where I'm heading. He can track me, just in case. And in the meantime, Bert'll let me know if anyone breaks into the apartment while I'm gone."

"You're gonna do this regardless, aren't you?"

"Yup."

"Ya know, if you weren't a temp, I'd have your ass for behaviour like this."

"Doesn't seem to bother Hanson any."

Hoove laughs then, relaxing a little. "Okay, fine. You get in touch with Carmichael, I'll message you with Donal's details."

"Thanks, Hoove."

"Just be careful," he replies and hangs up.

"Computer, dial Devin Carmichael, home number."

"Please wait..."

*Ring-ring. Ring-ring. Ring...*

"Caz, long time no hear. You gettin' yourself in trouble again?"

I roll my eyes, despite knowing he can't see me. "Unless you've stopped keeping your ear to the ground, you know full well what trouble I've gotten into."

"True enough, darlin'. So, how are you and the city's finest doing with the LVs?"

"How in the hell did you hear that so quickly?"

"Light Vamps, ya mean? I know a guy."

I sigh. "We're working on it. That's why I'm calling, anyway. I'm following some leads the PD can't. I don't suppose you know how I could get an audience with Saul Solomon, do you?"

"Now, there ain't anything the Kings can tell you that Donal O'Brien doesn't already know."

"I figured that. Like I said, though, the PD can't follow certain strings too easily. Unless he wants to out himself as having links to the dark side, he can't put anything in a report. Either that or he legitimately doesn't know."

"Keeping things careful, you understand, but why come to me? All things considered, you could have gone to a certain someone else."

"All things considered," I mimic, "I'd rather play it like I would if I wasn't in the position I am. Play by the rules, and you don't get booted from the game."

Devin considers this for a moment, then says, "Wise move. He'll like that. Okay, I ain't normally a conduit for this stuff, but I'll get something set up. Give me ten minutes, and I'll send you the details."

"Thanks, Devin, I'll sit tight until then."

"Talk to ya later."

Devin hangs up and I check my cell phone to see one new message from Hoove. As promised, he's given me Donal's cell number. I join Bert for a few minutes, watching out of the window, but I still see nothing. Eventually, Devin sends me the promised meeting details. I send him my thanks and give Donal a call. He answers after only one ring.

"You don't disappoint, do ya? I was hoping you'd do something like this."

"I thought you might be. You know where I'm heading?"

"The mall. First Contact Electronics," he replies.

"That's right. Just make sure you're ready to turn around. If Bert signals me, I'll let you know to head to mine."

"Aye, makes sense. You best get going."

I hang up without saying anything else. He's right, for a number of reasons. For one, if I'm keeping up with the façade that Fuerza is *not* all four Kings of Utah, then I need to treat this like it's real. That means having enough respect to turn up on time. For two, this is kinda going to be duplicate work, so I'd rather get it all done with and move on. "Bert. If anyone tries to break in, signal me on my cell phone. Also, don't attack the police if they turn up. Got it?"

"Caw."

I rub his head and say, "Back soon," then head for the door.

# Chapter Four

FIRST CONTACT ELECTRONICS is a mid-sized retailer on the first floor of the New Hopeland Mall. Looking for home appliances, entertainment devices, and general repairs? They've got you covered, at least according to the video sign in the main window. As per the instructions Devin sent me, I walk straight to the back of the store, and head for the security guard standing in front of the door to the staff area. As I approach, he nods, and I subtly hold four fingers pointing downward. The Four Kings of Utah are Brett Stantz, Gory Gutierrez, Saul Solomon, and Kerry White. Saul being the third King, I tuck my third finger under, leaving the first, second and fourth still visible. The guard nods again and waves me through the door. He leads me to the bottom of a stairwell and places his palm flat on the space just below one of the steps. A section of the concrete flashes and disappears, leaving a gap that opens into a dimly lit corridor.

I walk in when beckoned and note the glass sheet slides back into place behind me. That explains how no one noticed the holographic part of the steps; there's something solid behind it. The corridor only goes one way, and it isn't long, leading to a plain metal door only about thirty metres in.

I steel myself. This is where I need to be careful. I've gone to the effort of playing the game so far, and I have no idea how many people will be in this room, or how many of them will know that the four figureheads of Utah's criminal underworld, the people pulling all the strings, are in actuality one person: New Hopeland's lowest-rated wannabe gangster, Allen Fuerza. *Deep breath, Cassie, and here we go …*

The room beyond is simple. It's square shaped. There's a single wooden table in the middle, one chair in front of it, and a tablet on a stand sat on top of it. Two people flank the table, one male, one female, both wearing expensive suits and sunglasses. They both also have their guns on display, resting close to their hands, which are in turn crossed neatly in front of them. I walk slowly to the table and see that a message is displayed on the screen.

"PLACE YOUR WEAPONS ON THE TABLE"

I unholster the police issue HK first and place it on the table. Next, I take the Glock from its own holster, held higher than and on the opposite side to the police issue weapon. Just because it seems the right thing to do, I hold my hands up and do a slow turn for the two suits to indicate that this is it. The woman nods to the chair, and I take it as an invitation to sit down. Once I've done so, the screen flashes and I'm faced with Saul Solomon. He's wearing some sort of black Spandex covering over the top of his head, disguising his hair. On his face, he wears a white mask, featureless bar the eye holes and a simple crown illustration on one cheek. The crown, I note, has four prongs, and only the third features a jewel on top.

Sure, I've seen the man behind the mask—all the masks—but I've never actually seen any of the Kings. Even knowing what I do, it's an intimidating situation to be in. The whole setup *should* feel cartoony. But it doesn't. Last month, I met someone who works directly with the Kings. He was a shaven-headed man with a pair of sunglasses seemingly stuck permanently to his face. He was also clearly on par with Devin in terms of danger levels. Given that Devin is the city's legalised assassin, called in to clean up the messes others can't, it was a pretty scary experience. I'm getting a similar vibe from the two people watching me right now.

"Mr. Solomon," I say. "Thank you for agreeing to meet with me."

"How could I not?" replies a voice masked by a vocoder. "It is not often I am approached by someone outside my organisation. Tell me, Miss Tam, what brings a Private Investigator to my door?"

"I need information," I state plainly.

"There are plenty of people who would act as information brokers. Am I to assume this relates to me directly?"

"I'm afraid so. You will be aware, of course, that a Mr. Jack Stan was attacked recently. He is, I believe, in your employ."

"I am, and he is. What of it?"

"Are you aware of the nature of the attack?"

"Again, I am. As I understand it, the police were investigating the matter and deemed it to be a simple mugging."

"Officially, yes. Unofficially, they are aware that something more is happening."

"I see. And why have you come to me directly? I would imagine there are multiple victims in this instance."

Vocoder or not, there's no hiding the arrogance and self-assuredness there. He knows there are others, and he probably knows who's behind it all. He's just not acting on it. Nor is he going to tell me who it is. *Interesting.* "I'll cut to the chase, Mr. Solomon. I am working with the PD on the case. Having been a victim of the attacker myself, but one who got away without the attacker taking what he came for, there is a belief that I will be targeted again. As it stands, we're working to find out who the attacker is, and how they work. As such, I need to know... On the night he was attacked, was Mr. Stan on a job, or was he simply enjoying a night out at the theatre?"

Saul laughs out loud and replies, "Do you truly think I would tell someone working with the PD something like *that*?"

I shake my head. "Ordinarily, no. As it is, though, neither Mr. Stan nor you are targets of the investigation. On top of that, to our knowledge, Mr. Stan did not carry out any unlawful activity before he was attacked. We have no interest in whether he *did* complete a job, or even what the job is, we simply wish to know whether there *was* a job."

"Why?"

"Because, if there was, then we can start to approach this as a case of premeditated attacks. That makes it more likely the man responsible will try again, and we can start setting up false openings for him to do so."

"I will ask you one question, Miss Tam. Give me a satisfactory answer, and I will tell you what you want. Fail to do so, and this conversation is over."

I shiver involuntarily at the parallel to my final meeting with Allen Fuerza last month but manage a nod.

"Why should I help you *or* the PD with this case?"

I expected this question to come up. It was an obvious way not only for Fuerza to test me, but for him to make it look like there's good reason to hand over information in front of his goons. *Which pretty much confirms these two aren't in the know, or there'd be no need for the song and dance routine.*

"Because it is my belief that multiple victims have links to the Four Kings of Utah, and the likelihood of this being an accident is low. As a group, you work smartly. If the PD can resolve this without the need for you to move yourselves, it saves you from entering an unnecessary conflict."

Saul Solomon nods thoughtfully, and replies, "I have heard worse reasons to cooperate with others. Very well, as it is all you have asked to know, yes, Mr. Stan was on a job. Now, you may gather your weapons and return to your investigation."

I nod my thanks, get to my feet, and reholster both guns. Just before I open the door to leave, Solomon's voice calls out, "Oh, and Miss Tam? When you arrive home, you will find a piece of paper has been delivered. Should you have legitimate cause to contact the Kings, the preferred communication routes will be on there. Be warned, though. I do not expect such meetings to become commonplace."

I leave the room without saying another word. Once I get back to the stairwell end of the corridor, the security guard from earlier greets me with a surprised smile. I guess most people really *don't* come back from these meetings.

*Which just leaves Pauline Mensche.*


MY PHONE RINGS the moment I step outside the store, and the screen tells me it's Donal O'Brien. I tap the icon to answer and pull the phone up to my ear.

"So," he says. "Now ya know."

"I know Jack Stan was on a job, but nothing else. Is there more to it?"

"Nothing you'd be able to get outta a meeting like that, no. That was all you wanted to confirm, right?"

"Yeah," I concede. "I'll try to talk to someone about Pauline Mensche too. Even a little usable evidence is *something*, eh?"

"Aye, it is that."

I stop and lean against a nearby storefront, acting as casual as I can, just in case. "Have you spotted anyone I should be wary of?"

"Nah. Not having a description of the attacker when he's not suited up makes it difficult, ya know? So, I took a broad-brush approach."

"Meaning?"

"Used an old backdoor into the mall security systems. I've been streaming the cameras since you went in. Plenty of males walking around, but for the short time you were in there, only a few doubled back past the store. One stopped to look in through the window, entered the store, and hasn't come out again yet. I doubt he's anything more than a shopper, though. This guy's careful."

"That's assuming he really was following me."

"He ain't been caught yet. I'd say that makes him careful, even if he's not following you."

"True enough. I'm gonna go chase up the Mensche lead. I take it you're in the van again?"

"Best way to travel."

"Well...try to keep yourself out of sight. The Dealers have been keeping a low profile since that mess with Malcolm Castleford, and I don't want my contact getting spooked by a police van."

Donal snorts out a laugh down the phone. "They've only been keeping a low profile when it comes to the PD. They've been doing plenty of digging down below, not that they're gonna find anything. The best they've got at the moment is a bit of intimidation on Castleford himself. He's behaving, though, doing what he's told."

"Still, I don't want to risk this blowing up."

"Ah, it's fine. I'll keep us close enough to act, but far enough to hide, yeah?"

"Good. I'll be in touch."

I take one last look around in case there's anyone watching me that the camera's missed, or anyone who sets off a sense of recognition for me, but there's no one. Satisfied, I hop in a cab to Fenchurch Street.

CHARLOTTE GOLDMAN, CHARLIE for short, is one of the most successful Dealers in the city. She rose the ranks to Elite status within the organisation pretty quickly and has thus far avoided doing anything to draw police attention to herself. Or rather, she's been smart enough to keep her activities quiet when they've not been wrapped in a nice, cosy bundle of legal loopholes. For a long time, I only spoke to her when I needed something.

We were lovers, for a while at least, but we drifted apart over time and became more like friends trying awkwardly to be more than that. Even with it being amicable, I struggled with the split. Lori convinced me to get back into contact with her on a more regular basis, which has been great for the most part, but both Charlie and I have kept a little distance since the Castleford case. Being an accountant for a lot of people in the underground, the Dealers included, Malcolm Castleford going wild like he did set him up as a potential risk to Charlie and her colleagues. Charlie knows something's up, though. There was far too much noise being made for someone simply trying to screw over Allen Fuerza, especially as his reputation of being the biggest wannabe in Utah has remained intact.

*No time like the present to get things back on track*, I tell myself and give the doorbell a press. I put my hands in my pockets and have a look around while I wait. Fenchurch Street is a nice area for the most part. Quiet, well-maintained, all the usual stuff. It's also home to multiple people with their fingers in a bunch of pies, on the verge of falling into dodgy territory. Aside from Charlie, there are at least two company directors with a reputation for being overly secretive, a couple of self-titled online revolutionaries, and an alleged ex-marine with a body count longer than my arm. Most of the residents here are regular citizens, though.

The door clicks open and Charlie peers out at me, her face a picture of surprise. "Caz?"

"Hi, Charlie," I reply. "I know it's been a few weeks, but...sorry, is this a bad time?"

Charlie glances back into the house and pushes her unusually tousled auburn hair behind her ears. "Uhm...you know what? No, it's fine. Come in."

*Well, that's an odd reaction*, I note, following her in. When we get to the living room, I see that she has company. The woman in front of us is tall, or taller than me anyway, and has her raven-black hair tied back in a tight ponytail. She has a strong jawline that would classically have been regarded as masculine if it weren't for how much her smile softened it. I recognise her from the photos Charlie has up all around the house; it's her current girlfriend. Thinking about it, this is my first time meeting her in person.

"Sorry," I say, embarrassment creeping into my voice a little more than I expected. "I didn't mean to interrupt."

"No, no, it's all good," Charlie says, waving my concerns away. "Caz, this is Jody, Jody, Caz."

"Caz? Oh...Cassandra Tam, right?" Jody says, offering her hand.

I shake it and nod. She's letting me know that she knows who I am. That's fine. "Caz is fine. Or Cassie."

"Cassandra's for when you're getting told off by your parents, right?" she replies, smiling, and Charlie groans. Jody looks at her, slightly confused, and asks, "What?"

"I don't have the best relationship with my parents right now," I say, saving Charlie from having to try to explain it away. "My mom hasn't spoken to me in years, and Dad's..." I sigh. "Dad's no longer with us."

"Oh. Shit. I'm sorry, I didn't know."

I shake my head and smile as best I can. "No reason you *would* know. Don't worry about it."

"I'll make us some drinks." Charlie makes a beeline for the kitchen, leaving her current and ex partners alone in an awkward silence.

Eventually, Jody tries, "So, it must be interesting being a PI?"

I laugh. "That's one way to put it. It's not as exciting as you'd think most of the time. Lots of pouring over news links, CCTV footage, and stuff like that. When it's not like that, it's usually far too dangerous to be interesting."

"Wow," she replies, sounding genuinely impressed. "Beats me for action, hands down. I'm a DJ, so the worst I get is the odd drunk trying a little too hard to get my number, you know? I've seen your name on the news sites a few times, though, so you must be good, right? How come you went freelance rather than joining the police?"

"Oh, for fuck's sake," Charlie groans, frozen in the doorway with a tray of drinks and a plate of biscuits in her hand.

"What?" Jody asks, and I start to laugh. I shouldn't laugh. The subject is a sore one, and it hurts like hell to think about it, but this whole situation is so beyond comical at this point that I can't help it.

I give Jody the short version: I tried it and found myself in opposition to certain things, so Dad, a cop himself, helped me set up as a PI. He died protecting me when I dug too deeply into a case. By the time I've finished, I don't know what's worse; the genuine upset I'm keeping in, or the utter disbelief on Charlie and Jody's faces as I struggle to contain the laughter. "I...I'm sorry. It's just...of all the questions you could have asked."

"If I'd known you were coming, I'd have said something," Charlie says, her voice restrained but not quite hiding the flustered edge to it.

Jody, I notice, looks absolutely mortified. I compose myself, turn to her, and say, "Honestly, there's nothing to worry about. It's good to let it out sometimes. And like I said, there's no reason you would have known to avoid the subject."

"Okay," she says, relaxing a little, but still clearly annoyed with herself.

"So, what brings you here today?" Charlie asks.

I take a sip of my coffee. "Nothing too social, I'm afraid. You've seen the upturn in muggings?"

"Yeah, there's a lot of them going on at the moment. What about it?"

"I was one of the victims." Charlie starts to say something, but I put my hand up to stop her. "I'm fine, the attacker didn't actually get anything, but the police think that a couple of the cases may be linked. I'm kinda...helping piece it all together."

"Linked, huh?" Charlie replies, narrowing her eyes at me.

"Certain victims *may* have been stalked and picked up after a degree of planning," I clarify. "It's nothing more than that."

"And you're looking for evidence of the planning so that, what?"

"So they can set me up as bait to lure a second attack," I state plainly.

"Bait?" Charlie repeats. "Jeez, Caz, how'd you end up getting roped into that?"

"The same way you got to be warier around police involvement."

"Fucking Castleford," Charlie says, through gritted teeth.

"The accountant guy?" Jody asks.

"Yeah," I reply. "I got mixed up in that whole mess and...well...certain people don't care too much for me. Since they hold sway with the PD, it was *this* or prison time."

"Ugh," Charlie says, placing her mug onto the nearby coffee table in a far from delicate manner. "I swear, whatever Castleford found has been nothing but trouble for all of us. I take it you still can't tell me any more than you already have?"

I shake my head. "No. Not on that."

"*That's* stopping me from digging more myself. If it's spooked *you*, she with the shovel who just can't stop, then it's not worth the hassle. Okay, what do you need?"

I glance awkwardly at Jody and ask, "Is she...?"

"Don't worry," Jody says, getting to her feet. "I'm not sure I want to know what's going on here. New Hopeland's *almost* too scary for me to keep visiting as it is."

"Better get used to it," Charlie says with a smile. "I already told you I'm not moving."

Jody laughs and kisses Charlie's forehead. "I'll get the dinner on. Give me a shout when it's safe to come out."

I wait for her to leave the room, then turn to Charlie. "That serious, eh?"

"Yeah," she replies and holds up her hand to show a simple band on her ring finger. "Just got this last week. She asked if you're interested."

"Oh, wow," I say and try to shake off the surprise. "Well, congratulations."

"You're not upset at all?"

"No," I say, a genuine smile reaching my lips. "I'm happy for you. Honestly."

Charlie lets out a relieved sigh and shakes her head. She flashes me a cheeky smile and says, "I was actually kinda worried about telling you. Up until recently, you kinda still seemed like...well..."

"I had feelings for you?" I finish, and she nods. "I kinda did, but not like you're thinking. Even if part of me knew the end was coming for us, it still hit me hard. And yeah, that *was* why I didn't let anyone in for a while. There were things with you I just didn't let go of, and that's entirely because I didn't want to feel so damn alone all the time. If I still held on to some things, it meant things would be easier. Or I thought it would. It actually...screwed me up a little, I think."

"And now?"

"I still care about you, a lot, but not in the same way."

Charlie laughs quietly to herself, and asks, "Lori finally broke you, huh?"

"Some of my stubbornness at least," I reply, returning the laugh. "Look, if this is half as awkward for you as it is for me then...shall we get on with this?"

"Sure. What do you need?"

"Pauline Mensche was another of the victims. She was attacked shortly after purchasing Delta-S. I need to know who she bought from and whether they'd be willing to answer some questions for me."

"Pauline Mensche...she's Brett Stantz's thief," Charlie muses. "Delta-S is only ever distributed to two Dealers at once, one Elite and one other. I was the Elite this month, but I only made one sale of the stuff. It's pretty potent, so we only ever make bigger sales to people taking it outside for further dispersion. My sale was like that. You've met the other seller, though. L3G3ND."

"The guy with the gold chains and the crappy beard?"

"That's the one," Charlie laughs. "And *he* says it's a cool beard. Hang on a minute." She pulls her cell phone out and dials a number. I hear someone answer on the other end of the line and start yammering away. Eventually, Charlie rubs her eyes, and cuts him off with an abrupt, "L, will you shut up and listen for a minute." She waits to make sure he's silent, then continues, "Did you sell some Delta-S to Pauline Mensche recently...? Okay, good. You remember Cassie Tam, right? I've got her here right now, and she needed to ask some questions about the deal...no, nothing like that...no, Pauline had some trouble afterwards, and she's...no, not with the DS, something else. Look, I'm putting you on speakerphone. Be nice, and tell her what she wants, yeah?"

Charlie places her phone on the table and taps the speaker icon, and L3G3ND's voice immediately cuts in with, "Can't be serious, c'mon, Chazza."

"Hi, Legend," I say.

"Aww, damn it," he snaps abruptly. "Hello, Cassie. It's L-3-G-3ND, remember?"

"Bit of a mouthful, don't'cha think?"

"Yeah, well, that's what she said. Whadda ya want?"

"I think I preferred you when you were being more cooperative. It's like *Chazza* said," I reply, responding to Charlie's wince at her nickname with a knowing grin. "I have a few questions about the Pauline Mensche deal. Nothing incriminating. It's more about Pauline herself."

The Dealers' only jumble of numbers and inappropriate capitalisation goes silent for a moment, seemingly thinking it over, then says, "Okay, yeah. I can work with that. But I ain't gonna answer anything that could land me in it.

"No problem. When Pauline came to you, had she arranged the deal in advance?"

"She'd checked I had stock, but that was the same day. Next question."

"Welcome to the lightning round," I grumble to myself. "Okay, when she came by, did she seem paranoid at all?"

"Paranoid in what way?"

"Glancing over her shoulder a lot, staring out the window, that sort of thing. Or did she maybe mention someone following her?"

"Yeah, yeah, yeah. Lots of checking out the window. That ain't unusual, though. You know what Delta-S is, right? It's a hallucinogen. For most people, it's a pretty nice trip, but the comedown's weird. First day or so is nothing more than a hangover, if you get anything at all. The paranoia kicks in after that. Unless they've got foresight, most people don't buy more until they hit the worst part of the comedown. That's the beauty of it, right? That paranoia makes them crave more so they can relax."

"Okay, but did she mention someone following her? Or watching her?"

"A couple of times, yeah, but like I said, it's normal for D-S users. Next question."

I roll my eyes and ask, "Has she bought from you before?"

L3G3ND harrumphs to himself then answers, "A couple of times, yeah."

"And is she normally someone who buys when the aftereffects have already kicked in?"

"No. But you gotta understand, she's not a long-time user. Just 'cause she got it right at the start don't mean she can't screw up. All this means is the powder's got its claws into her properly now. Next question."

"Nah, you've given me enough," I say, then reach out and hang up before he can say anything else to annoy me. I smile at Charlie and start, "Thanks, Chaz—"

"Don't you dare," she interjects, cutting me off before I can use her new nickname.

My phone *beeps* in my pocket, and I pull it out. I take one look at the screen, and say, "I gotta go."

"Already?"

"Yeah, give me a moment." I quick dial Donal and as soon as he answers, I say, "Bert just let me know there's an emergency at the apartment. You better get over there."

"We're one block away from you, on Taunston. Want us to wait for you?"

"Yeah, that'd be good." I hang up and start to make a move for the door. "Sorry to cut this short, but it sounds like the repeat attack is starting."

"No, no. You better get going or Bert won't leave enough of them to question. You need a ride?"

"Thanks, but no. I've got a shadow from the PD out on Taunston Street, just in case I got attacked here. They'll get me there. Oh, and sorry about that. I told them to hold back rather than come across like they were checking up on you."

"Don't worry about it." Charlie opens the door for me, and adds, "Stay safe."

"Will do. And congratulations again. We'll have to set up a double date sometime."

"Sure, sounds fun."

I give a quick wave and take off towards Taunston. When I get there, Donal swings the back door of the van open and says, "Cab for Miss Tam?"

"Sounds good to me," I reply and jump in.

The van takes off down the street, and I start to check over both the Glock and the HK45. Glancing up, I can see Donal flex-testing his claws and snout. He's been suited up for a long time. He must be glad to finally see some action.

By the time we reach my floor on the apartment block, there are already a couple of people standing around and staring at my door, listening to the angry "Caw, caw," of the Familiar inside. Given the noise, it's safe to say we don't have the element of surprise, so I brace myself and charge shoulder first at the door, forcing it open. I immediately draw the HK45 and step to the side, making room for Donal to enter behind me while I try to take in what I'm seeing.

The kitchen sink is running on full power, the water pouring out with force from the remnants of the nozzle. The rest of it? Trapped between the beak of the little metal gargoyle that seems intent on telling it off for making a mess.

I walk calmly through the mass of water soaking my floor and turn the faucet off, noting not only the slight indentations caused by metal claws, but the plug that has slid into place. Once the water stops, Bert drops the chunk of metal from his mouth, and gives a triumphant, "Caw."

"Sorry, excuse me," comes a voice from the doorway, and an elderly man pushes past Donal without batting an eyelid. "Ah, you've sorted it then."

"Sorted what?" I ask, recognising our block's handyman, Mr. Thorne.

"Power surge caused some of the electronic appliances to go haywire. I've been working up each floor to stop anything going off where the residents were out. You're back now, though, and you've stopped...ah, the faucet. Yes, two others on the third floor had the same issue. Plug slid in automatically and the water started running. I see ol' Bert had a crack at fixing it too, didn't he?"

I smile and stare at the damage. "Yeah. Yeah, he did."

"Well, I'll be off then," says Mr. Thorne, stopping only to look Donal up and down and comment, "You're a big fella, aren't you?"

"This sorta thing happen often?" Donal asks.

"Sometimes," I say and give Bert a pat. "Good try, Bert."

Bert's initial attempts may have stemmed the flow long enough to prevent too much water escaping the confines of the sink. Ripping the nozzle off probably didn't help in the way he intended, but it did at least crush the remaining pipe enough to keep the spray slower than it would have been otherwise. In all, he really did more good than harm in this instance. I pull a drawer open and rummage through some random-and-far-too-small-for-my-liking tools that came with various appliances I've owned. The little metal rod that works as a reset tool for the sink eventually comes to hand, and I slip it into the gap at the back of the faucet set, causing the plug hole to open with a *clunk*. The water is draining fine, so that's a good sign.

"I'll see if I can find something to mop this up with," I say, and head off to my bedroom. It's a strange place to go, but I *think* I left a towel in there that would make a good starting point. I spot the blue fabric of one of the older towels slumped under the window. "No use hiding," I tell it, and out of habit, glance out through the venetian blinds. I freeze.

"Got you..."

Slowly, I back away from the window, dropping the towel on my bed as I make my way into the main room. "Bert, stay here, unless I signal you. Donal, we need to get moving. He's here."

Understanding what I mean instantly, Donal nods and walks out of my apartment. I pull the door shut on my way through.

I EXPLAIN THE plan to Donal on the way down in the elevator. It all hinges on the LV having stayed around the back of the building and so not seeing Donal with me, but given Bert's previous sentry position, that seems like a good bet.

Once we hit the ground floor, I make my way out of the building alone, turning right to head around the back where I saw my stalker. I struggle to contain a smile when I notice him waiting for me, still only half hidden in the shadows of an alley. Once he's sure he's got my attention, he turns and walks slowly into the dark. Like the idiot he clearly thinks I am, I follow.

Unlike the last time we met, this alley is short, and the street lights at the other end provide enough illumination to allow me to see where I'm going. It also lets me see the door swinging open towards the back of the alley, on the opposite side of the apartment block I thought Bert had been watching earlier. What is this place, again? A storage area, I think, for one of the local convenience stores. Coming up to the door, I catch a glimpse of the damaged wires and scraps of metal inside the frame, showing where my attacker has had to break in. *Someone's been busy setting this up,* I note, spotting the equally damaged security camera above me.

Inside, I realise I'm right. The building is spacious enough, but the crates and boxes that have been pushed out towards the wall all bear the markings of various popular suppliers. To my right is a light switch, but of course, my casual flicking of it does nothing. I expected that, though. I sigh, and shake my head, then walk further into the room.

"Okay, *I* know you're in here, and *you* know that I know it. Let's get this over with."

I hear a shuffling to the side. Taking the bait, I walk into the middle of the room and turn to face the source of the sound. Someone steps out of the shadows. At first, he is nothing more than a shadow. As my eyes begin to adjust, I start to make out details. The shiny, visored mask looks like the sort of thing you'd see in a video game, the kind worn in sci-fi shooters. It's covered in smooth, blackened glass that covers and hides the whole face. The side of the helmet has two stylised chunks of metal resembling ears. Or maybe antenna.

*Could that be what's picking up the signals from the trackers?* My hand goes to the lump in my neck. I barely have time to recognise the long, claw-like fingers, or the dark robe he's wearing, before the fangs at the bottom of the mask light up and start flashing. Once again, fear overwhelms me, and my legs start to shake.

"No," I growl, trying desperately to stay upright. I unholster the HK45, but my arm is shaking too much for it to get a clear aim on the advancing... *Vampire. He is a vampire.* I drop the gun to the floor and grab for the Glock instead. I swing it out in front of me and squeeze the trigger, hoping that instinct has been kind. The bullet makes a loud *thud* as it hits a crate, several feet behind my attacker.

I catch a movement out of the corner of my eye and allow myself a slight smile as I drop to the floor, the gun sliding from my fingers. The vampire draws closer and lowers himself to one knee in front of me. I groan, and spit the slurred words, "Got you, you son of a bitch."

A loud crash of metal cuts through the *put-put-put* of the flashing fangs, as Donal O'Brien barrels into my would-be attacker. They tumble to the floor and, with the light away from my face, I try to clear the cobwebs, listening intently to the sounds around me. My vision fades in and out a little, but I catch glimpses of the ensuing battle.

Donal grabs the vamp and slams him against a crate.

The vamp slams a chunk of wood between the jaws of Donal's snapping muzzle, and barges him back, tearing his own cloak off in the process.

My mind is screaming something at me, but I'm still too hazy to make it out. I'm missing something. Something important.

Donal rights himself and takes a swipe at the vamp's shoulder, then swings his other arm across to grab him by the mask when he tries to dodge.

My head finally clears just as the vamp aims his fangs directly at Donal's eyes and alters the pattern of the flashing. "Ain't gonna work anymore, ya little bastard," Donal grunts, and smashes a metal-coated fist into them, shattering the glass. "You're coming with…"

Suddenly, everything falls apart.

The fear comes back, and I'm sent tumbling to the floor again as a new wave of dizziness hits. All around me, the shadows are moving, twisting into the familiar shapes of people, pointing and watching. Worst of all, it's hit Donal too. The big Irishman has released the vampire and dropped to his knees, his body spasming as he coughs up bile that sticks to and hangs from his razor-sharp teeth.

I can hear my voice muttering incoherently as I desperately fumble for the Glock. Before I know it, there's the familiar sensation of a gloved hand wrapping around my throat and forcing me face down to the floor. "There's no light," I moan and close my eyes.

*Crack.*

The hand slips from my throat, and I roll over to see the vampire spin and flail an arm across his head, swiping Bert out of the air and sending him crashing into a nearby crate. My head starts to clear again, and my hand finally finds the Glock, just as an enraged Donal O'Brien lunges at our foe. The vampire sidesteps and I take aim, but he moves quicker, leaping into the air. A loud *pop* echoes around the room, followed by a *crunch*, and the vampire seems to push off the air to get height. Another *pop* and *crunch*, and he sails higher still, breaking through a window at the opposite end of the room.

I collapse to the floor, breathing heavily, and ask out loud. "You okay, Bert?"

"Caw," he replies, hopping down from the crate he'd landed in. Or through. Looking over at him, I notice his left wing has snapped in two. And the remnant is dragging behind him in his hand.

"Thanks for the concern," Donal says, offering me a hand. I take it and let him pull me to my feet.

"Well, that went well," I grumble. "What now?"

"Now, we get the rest of the team in here and see if we can salvage anything useful from this mess."

HANSON AND DEVEREAUX are on the scene within twenty minutes, which is a testament to either there being a low volume of traffic tonight, or to whichever one of them was the driver knowing the best routes. "No Hoove?" I ask.

"He's sticking back for now," Devereaux replies. "He said that if any more attacks come through, he'd rather someone in the know was at the station to handle it."

"So, what have we got?" Hanson cuts in, making her way back into the room. "Donal said the eye covering didn't work?"

"It did," I say. "At first at least. Come to think of it, Donal smashed the guy's fangs. There's no way the light caused the second wave."

"Could they have had an accomplice?" Devereaux tries. "Maybe someone else shone the light at you the second time?"

I shake my head. "I'd have noticed it. Plus, the glass worked for Donal at first. If there was someone else using the same equipment, even if it was in a different way, it shouldn't have hit him like that. This was different, anyway."

"Different how?" Hanson asks, inspecting a cracked indentation that's appeared in the floor.

"The dizziness was similar, and the fear was the same. I didn't feel sick this time, though. There were some... hallucinations."

"Like what?"

I shrug. "It's kinda hazy. But the crates all sorta twisted into people. They were just standing there, watching, but it was freaky."

Footsteps from the door cause us all to turn, and we see Donal O'Brien entering the room. He's changed out of the TS gear and is now in a more comfortable looking pair of tracksuit bottoms and a vest top. Hanson smiles and says, "Cassie says the glass worked against the lights."

"Not the second time, it didn't."

"There was no light the second time," I reiterate.

"There had to be something," he grumbles. "What've ya got there, Hanson?"

"Remember how you said the LV *flew* out the window? I think I've figured out how. Hold on." Hanson runs her fingers over the indentation in the floor, and asks, "Did he seem unusually tall at all? Or did he look like he had lifts in his boots?"

"Can't say I was paying attention," Donal replies.

"He was shorter than Donal in his gear," I say. "But taller than me."

"Hmmm," Hanson mumbles and starts searching to her left. She picks up a piece of twisted metal from the floor and waves it at us. "He did the flying thing twice, right?"

"He wasn't really flying," I clarify. "It was more like he was jumping in the air."

Hanson nods and makes her way across the room, pulling a torch from her belt to provide some extra light. She finds a second indent nearer the window that was used for the escape and soon has another piece of twisted metal in her hand. She nods at Donal and asks, "That compressed air upgrade you were trying to get funded? The one to give you extra height and speed when you jump? I think he used a similar system. These would have been on the base of his boots. Once he was as high as he could go, he'd have launched them at the floor, probably with a release of air. The force and the reduction in weight would have given him a boost, mid-jump."

I take one of the pieces of metal and turn it over in my hands. "This would have only added a couple of inches to his height, so I doubt we'd have noticed lifts if we were looking. It doesn't feel like much of a weight reduction either."

"The boots would have needed a release system too," Hanson replies. "Having them anywhere other than the sole of the foot would risk it snapping upwards during use, so you can probably add a few more inches for that. In other words, he has tech-filled platforms. Oh, and the compressed air would play into the weight reduction too. Old style scuba tanks contained three kilograms of air. We can compress three or four times that into smaller air boxes now. Release it all in one go, and you'd get quite a kick. He must do some killer legwork to haul that around, though."

"That would explain the sound," I say, still studying the metal intently.

Devereaux frowns. "Sound?"

"Like a pop, and a smack. The air release, and the metal hitting the ground."

"Makes sense," Donal replies. "Is Shift Source Ltd still the only one working on the system?"

"Dunno," Hanson shrugs. "We can always check with Dean Hollister. He likes to keep an eye on competitors, so he'd know if anyone else could do it. And if not, we'll check his sales."

"Or have a suspect," Devereaux adds.

Hanson shrugs again.

I feel a slight pull on my leg as Bert starts to clamber up me to perch on my shoulder. I've got the folded remains of his wing tucked into my trousers so that he can move about a bit easier, which seemed to make him happy. He's been rummaging around the crate he hit since the others got here, though, and once he gets himself comfortable I learn why. He drops something from his beak, and I barely catch it in time.

"Bring your torch over here," I say, and Hanson does so. Bert has given me a thick, pointy lump of something. It feels like heavyweight plastic in my hand, and it's pitch black, like the LV's helmet.

"Is that one of its ear things?" Donal asks.

"Could be," I say. "Looks pretty damaged. Think we can get anything from it?"

"We could try to check if it really is receiving the tracker signals," Devereaux suggests, taking it from my hand. "Even if we can't get it working properly, if the insides are at least recognisable, we could trace its use through the different parts."

"Thanks, Bert," I say, and he clicks contentedly in my ear. I look up at the rest of the team and add, "Sorry to have to do this, but I better head home. Even without *this*, my kitchen is still flooded. I'm gonna need to sort that."

"Yeah, it did look a state," Donal chuckles.

"It's fine," Devereaux replies. "We can finish up here, eh?"

"Sure," Hanson says, and nods at Donal. "You should go rest too. We're gonna need you at your best if we get another shot at this guy."

Donal nods his agreement and follows me out of the building. He winks as he walks by and says, "See? Time alone together for the lovebirds," then trots off towards the van.

I shake my head, a bemused smile on my face, and make my way back to the apartment block. Mr. Thorne greets me at the main entrance. "Ah, good. He found you then. He was scratching at the door when I came back down, and since I'd seen you leaving through one of the windows, I thought I should let him out. He'd only use the window otherwise."

I smile. "He would, that. Thank you, Mr. Thorne. Say thanks, Bert."

"Caw."

"You're very welcome," he replies. "If you need any help cleaning up the water, let me know."

"We should be fine, but thanks again," I say, and head for the elevator. Once we're back home, I shut the door and put Bert's broken wing on the work desk.

"Computer, open server six, primary folder case files, subfolder Orlok, subfolder personal notes. Open file notes. Activate dictation."

"Dictation activated, please confirm text."

I grab the towel and start mopping up the remaining water, as I speak. "The glass covering protected Donal from the light, confirming the theory about how the attacker carries out their attacks. The second wave had no clear indicator of source. It *did* cease after Bert intervened, though, so it obviously requires some form of direct involvement from the attacker. It's interesting that the technology used to allow him to jump is potentially Shift Source Limited produced. More interesting is that Hanson didn't seem convinced Dean Hollister is a potential suspect. I wonder why she's against that as a possibility. End dictation and save."

"File saved."

*I'll have to take Bert in for repairs tomorrow. I could try getting him in tonight...no. Right now, I feel better having him around.*

# Chapter Five

I OPEN MY eyes in a darkened room.

A single light bulb swings freely on a chain, and the gentle *clink-clink* of the movement is the only sound I can hear. I try to say something but find that my mouth has been gagged with what feels like an old rag. Not one to be so easily silenced, I lift my hands to remove it, but I can't. My hands have been forced into a prayer position and bound with something. It only takes me a moment to notice the weight on my wrists and hear the metallic clunking going on around me, not to mention how the light is swaying a little more than before.

Concentrating, I start pulling my arms back and forth until I start to fall off balance. Feeling the pressure below, I plant my feet solidly on the floor and lean back, maintaining my seated position but yanking my arms towards me until the bulb starts to swing more freely. The light intermittently catches where I want it to and confirms a few things for me. First, my feet are chained together. Second, my hands have been bound with several layers of electrical tape, and also wrapped in a chain, the length of which runs under the one attached to my feet, and up towards the swinging light bulb.

A few more test pulls show there's something stopping me from yanking the chained light free. It also means that if I get to my feet, I won't have enough chain to stand up straight.

*Well, that's inconvenient. Okay, Cassie, let's sort out that gag.*

I snap my mouth and grind my teeth against the fabric, trying to bite my way through, but I can't tell whether I'm making any real headway. All thoughts of persistence cease when I spot something in the shadows ahead. I concentrate in front of me and gently pull my arms like I'm threading rope through a loop above my head. The bulb starts to swing and, as the light hits where I'm staring, my blood runs cold.

The Light Vamp is standing in the room, his head angled towards me. The swaying light intermittently reflects off the blackened visor that covers his face, and I catch sight of the two ear-like protrusions on the side of the helmet, and the number 49 printed on his forehead. At the base of the helmet, the shattered remains of his fangs look almost menacing. Rather than the pitiful mess of mangled of lighting they are, they seem like war wounds; scars of a battle that neither of us truly won.

The light bulb starts to glow a little brighter, giving me flashes of the LV's body. Without the cloak, the shiny skintight bodysuit he's wearing is clearly visible. No, wait. Make that *she's* wearing. This vamp is female. With the cloak no longer masking her form, I can see the heavy bracing running up over her thick boots and snaking up a pair of muscular thighs. The strapping stops at her waist, taking on the appearance of a belt, sitting snugly above her hips. Her arms feature a similar strapping, snaking out the back of thick gloves built to extend the fingers like claws. Her body looks as if it's covered in panels, likely to provide protection, both to her and the tech she's using.

I don't have time to think.

The vampire rattles her nails together, and all of a sudden, the room is full of sound. I start pulling my arm chain to the side, and the bulb swings wildly. As the light illuminates the sides of the room, I see rows of dogs, each a pitch-black Doberman, chained to the walls. They struggle against their collars, howling and barking as though they're in pain.

A shadow moves across me and I look up.

The vampire is now right in front of me, looming over me like a lion that has finally captured its prey.

She lunges.

I SIT UP in bed, panting heavily as cold sweat pours down my face. Even as realisation slides into place, I pull my hand up to my face and rub at my eyes, trying to tear the images away.

Over the years, I've learned to pay attention to my dreams when it comes to cases. Often, what my waking mind can't see, my subconscious can show me in my sleep. The problem here is that it may not apply. I've seen the LV as a movie monster from the get-go, and last night's confrontation certainly didn't help dispel that.

"And what do movie monsters give you?" I grumble to myself. "Nightmares."

*But why was the vamp in my dream female? We already established that the attacker was male.*

I shake my head and push my hair back out of my face. Determined not to let the fear get the better of me, I haul myself out of bed and shower quickly, then cook up a couple of sausages to shove between some over-buttered slices of bread for breakfast. Once I've eaten, I call Familiar Enterprises Limited and arrange to drop Bert in for repairs, giving a brief description of the damage, but nothing more. I'll go through the security issues when I get there.

Looking at the time, it's not quite late enough that I can guarantee everyone else being at the station yet. Now, whose number do I have who likely won't be rolling in for the early shift? I smile, and say, "Computer, activate speaker phone and dial Lieutenant Hanson, Mobile Number."

"Please wait…"

I take another mouthful of greasy goodness—the only reason I'm using the speaker system rather than my actual cell phone right now—and wait. After a few seconds, the ringing gives way to a bemused sounding Hanson. "Someone's eager this morning." She laughs, then adds, slightly muffled, "Not you."

"Busy?" I ask.

"Nah, it's just Dev mucking around."

I smile to myself, and reply, "I was gonna see if you were up to a quick trip, but I feel bad asking now."

"Nah, don't feel bad. I've got a slightly later start today anyway. Plus, I'm way better company than any of the local cab drivers."

"You'll get no arguments there."

"Yup. And you *can* just come straight out and ask for a ride. We're partners on this case, and after last night, it makes sense that we all stick close. Where did you need to go?"

"The FE Limited building. Bert's gonna need some repairs, and I'm gonna have to explain a few things to them. Shouldn't take too long, but if it's gonna be too far out of the way, just say, and I'll harass the cab companies."

"Sounds fine to me. I'll drop Dev at the station then swing by yours. Think you can be ready in about an hour?"

"Absolutely. Thanks, Hanson."

"No problem. See you in a bit."

Hanson hangs up and I can't help but smile again. "I guess Donal was right."

I tap my fingers on the table. "An hour... I guess that's enough time to file my report."


"SO. DEV, HUH?" I say, pulling myself into the front seat of Lieutenant Hanson's car. Bert is strapped into one of the backseats in power down mode, ready for his wing reattachment.

She laughs, checks the road, and pulls out. "No judging, you. If *you* can date clients, *I* can date colleagues."

"True enough. It surprised me, is all. He seems so innocent."

"And you're saying I'm not?" She smirks, knowing full well I won't buy that.

"Three words. Black Widow tattoo."

"I'll have you know Suzy Spindle Legs is a classy lady."

"Classy? What was it you told me? That they used to call you the Black Widow in college because nobody who dated you was emotionally able to date anyone else after you were done with them? That you'd essentially killed everyone's chances with them? Oh, and let's not forget you got the tattoo while drunk because you were *proud* of the achievement."

Hanson laughs and replies, "Okay, one, I was young. Two, I'm sure my exes are all fine now. Mostly. Three, the art is fucking good. And four, Dev happens to find that story funny. Besides, he's sweet. That's fun to dick with."

"Poor Corporal Devereaux..." I say, shaking my head.

"I had a similar thought about you when I saw you in Tourniquet. Didn't seem like your normal sort of haunt."

I shrug. "Not really, but that was more due to my own misconceptions than anything. Nice people."

"Yeah. I don't get out there much these days, but they're a good lot."

"Just been busy?"

"Yeah. Cases have been coming my way thick and fast of late. But hey, what can you do?"

I nod. "Before I forget, there was something I wanted to ask you."

"Still not telling you my first name," Hanson replies, giving me a cheeky wink.

"Not *that*," I laugh. "It was to do with the test on Donal's TS gear. What was that you were doing with the dazzlers?"

"Just messing around really."

I raise my eyebrows and furrow my brow. "Bullshit. I recognised the kata from some TV demonstration. That was Krav Maga knife work."

"It was and it wasn't. There were some other techniques in there too, but yeah, it was mostly Krav Maga. It's not a police thing, though, so as Hoove keeps telling me, it's officially known as messing around."

"I know the academies used to do a mix of boxing, grappling, and pressure point work. Still, I can't picture Hoove objecting to one of his officers knowing how to defend themselves?"

"He doesn't really, as long as I don't spend time practising that *should* be spent on a case. Donal's the only other one in the station who knows it, so he gets to be my crash test dummy more often than not. There were a few others, rookies mostly, but they didn't seem to enjoy me using them as test subjects too much."

"I can imagine. Krav Maga's a military martial art. I think it's...Israeli, isn't it? How'd you come to learn it?"

Hanson laughs. "Sambo's a military martial art too, and there's a school two blocks from you."

I roll my eyes. "I know you would have gone to a training school. I meant when, and why?"

"I know what you meant, I just like messing with you. I learned it a few years before I came to New Hopeland. It was pretty much all everyone learned martial arts-wise around my way. Useful stuff, though."

"I bet. You look a lot better at that than I do with...well, anything I've trained in, really."

"Did you not take any martial arts up when you were younger then? I figured you would have."

"Oh yeah? And why's that?" I tease. "Because I look like a Hong Kong movie star?"

"Cheeky. Nah, I just thought that being the daughter of a cop and having gone through the academy, you'd have a background in something, is all."

I shake my head. "I got the basics done, but I'm a bit rough around the edges. I was all right with boxing, but even then, I'm a long way from pro level."

"Well, if you ever want to learn something new, let me know. I'd be happy to teach you a few things. Your girlfriend too if she's up for it."

"I don't know about Lori, but I may take you up on that some time. No harm in upskilling, eh?"

We pull into the parking lot, and Hanson sits back into her seat. "I'll stick around out here. That way, if you start taking too long, I can just sneak off to work before you notice."

"Why does part of me think you're only half joking?" I reply, grabbing Bert and making my way through the front doors of the building.

For the second time in as many visits, I'm ushered up to the third floor. This time, rather than the kindly receptionist, I'm greeted immediately by Doctor Faraday. "Miss Tam. I understand there has been another issue with Bert. Of a physical nature this time?"

"That's one way to put it," I reply, and follow the doctor into her office. "No Brenda today?"

"Part-time hours. Today is her late start day. Now, I see you have Bert in power down mode. That's good. If I could?"

I hand Bert over to her and pull the broken wing out of the small bag I have it in, placing it on the table next to him. Doctor Faraday turns him around and examines the remnants of his left wing on his body, lightly pulling it up and down.

"It still seems flexible...no visible damage to the smaller structures associated with movement." She picks up the broken wing and turns it over a few times. "The denting indicates a heavy impact, though not from an object travelling towards Bert. He collided with something?"

"He was thrown," I reply, and Doctor Faraday raises an eyebrow at me.

"I'm sorry? If his wing was open, he was undoubtedly in the process of a protection protocol. For someone to be able to throw him in this state is...unusual, shall we say?"

I nod. "Okay, before I continue, I need to make you aware that I'm working a case with the police at the moment. What happened, happened during an operation. How far will what I tell you, or what you find when working on Bert, go?"

"Ah, you ask of us what we asked of you. Our guidelines ensure that confidentiality is paramount. There are many potential uses for the Familiar Project moving forward, and so we have enshrined a lot of safety measures into our working practices in readiness. All you tell me, and all I find during the repair and diagnostics, will be treated the same as any other case you have worked on with him."

"Meaning?"

"Material that requires it will be censored in our records, and none but myself and, if required, Mr. Burrell, will be made aware of the nature of the events."

"Okay, good enough. I and a member of the PD's Tech Shifter Unit were tackling a suspect. The suspect had the upper hand, so Bert stepped in. While he *did* cause the attack to cease, Bert was thrown by the suspect and collided with a crate."

"I see... Did you request that he record anything during the operation?"

"No. I wasn't actually expecting him to join us."

"In that case, your concerns around confidentiality are unfounded. During the repairs, I will extract the internal behavioural and memory logs he keeps as a standard part of his operation, just in case anything is of use to you and the police in your enquiries. These will be low on detail, however, so are likely to be, frankly, useless to you."

"No harm in checking," I reply. "Shall I leave him here with you, then?"

"Yes, unless you have booked him in with another technician and intended this as a social call."

"Humour. Nice touch," I say, but Doctor Faraday doesn't smile. I get to my feet with a sigh. "Well, let me know when he's ready for pickup."

When I make it back down to the car, Hanson pushes the door open and asks, "All okay?"

"Yeah. No issues with confidentiality, and they'll get straight on to working on him."

"Good. We just had a call from the Captain. We're to meet with Dean Hollister in the SSL offices, then head to the station. Apparently, Doctor Sanderson may have found something."

"MISS HANSON," DEAN Hollister says. "And Miss Tam too? It has been a while."

"A few months," I say, taking his outstretched hand and giving it a firm shake.

"Quite. Do you see much of Miss Redwood at all? I was wondering if the maintenance work helped with the issues she was having with Ink. Ah, but then, I suppose there would be little reason for you to keep in contact after the case, would there?"

"We're still in touch," I reply. "She seemed impressed with the work, and Ink hasn't fallen apart or anything, so I'd say it was a success."

"Good, good," he says and turns his attention to Lieutenant Hanson. "Now, I understand you had some questions regarding one of our systems. If you'd kindly step this way."

The last time I was here, I met with Dean Hollister on the top floor of the building. This time, we're on the third of ten underground floors, which contains one of SSL's in-house testing facilities. Looking around me as we walk, it's clear that the staff are busy. I can see a few leg sections being worked on, and large groups gathered around computers and whiteboards, discussing something no doubt important to the Tech Shifting system.

Hollister leads us into a small office at the back of the room and points us to some chairs. He sits down and straightens out his suit—which is far better fitting this time,

I note—and offers an apologetic smile. "My apologies for not taking you up to my main office. The view there is rather spectacular, as I'm sure Miss Tam can attest. Unfortunately, we've got a fair few tests to run through today, so I'm needed down here."

"Anything interesting?" Hanson asks, and Hollister shrugs.

"That rather depends on your point of view. We're experimenting with new brands of bolts and lubricant."

Hanson smiles and replies, "Not my sorta thing, I'm afraid."

"Such is life. I must say, though, I was not expecting to see Miss Tam here today." He turns his head to me and asks, "Are you now working with the city's finest?"

"Only on this," I reply. "I have a...vested interest, shall we say?"

"I see, I see. So, what can I do for you both?"

"We've been tracking someone," Hanson replies. "He's pretty tooled up in terms of tech, and when Cassie tackled him last night, he did something that sounds like it ties in with one of your recently announced projects."

"Which one?"

"Boost jumping."

"Ah," he sighs and hunches over slightly. "And what makes you believe this to be the case?"

"When I fought this person," I say, "he made his escape through a high window. He jumped, there was a loud pop, and he jumped again, another pop, and another jump, all while still in the air."

"I found this too," Hanson says, pulling out one of the mangled metal pieces she found at the storage building.

Hollister turns the lump over in his hand a few times and says, "It looks like a twisted shoe. Or the sole of one, rather."

"Looks like a lump to me," I comment.

"It does if you've never seen one before," Hollister replies, nodding. "This was the result of many of our earlier tests, however."

"Only the earlier ones?" Hanson asks.

"Yes. You see, the promotional material we put out describes the process quite simply. The general idea is that the boost system uses conservation of momentum to create the effect of mid-air jumps. Reducing weight is an important part of the process but testing this is difficult when using the main system. We work entirely with compressed air now that we know the system works, but metal was, and still is, cheaper than compressed air."

Hanson clicks her tongue. "So, when you were in the testing stage, you used what? Fifty per cent metal weight and 50 per cent air weight?"

"It varied throughout the process," Hollister confirms. "The metal system worked well enough, but launching chunks of it at the floor at high speeds? That left too much potential for damage liability, especially as it pertained to the damage of other humans. Of course, the air still carries some of this risk, which is why the system was only ever conceived for enforcement use, but it is reduced somewhat."

"So, it was never intended for public use," I say, thinking out loud. "Could we be looking at someone within an enforcement organisation then?"

Hollister shakes his head. "Not with one of our products. Aside from the official release date not having been reached yet, as I said, our product is now compressed air only."

"How long has the project been in the works?" I ask.

"I'd guess about five months," Hanson replies. "Donal's been on about it since the press release three months ago, and there would have to be a run-on from conception to certainty of potential workability, right?"

"You are near enough correct," Hollister says, giving Hanson an impressed smile. "We normally have a much longer gap, but this was simply an addition to the currently available gear."

"Not to mention that the science behind it is fairly simple compared to some of the bigger projects," Hanson adds.

"May I ask," Hollister says. "Is the man you're searching for a Tech Shifter?"

"No," I reply.

Hollister strokes his bottom lip, a thoughtful look on his face. "In a way, I am relieved to hear that, as it means the screening system is still working. On the other hand, if he had been a Tech Shifter, we could have checked sales to see if we could find a match."

"You keep sales records in that much detail?" I ask.

"Oh, yes. Conceptual art and photos of the TS gear, and photos, basic details and screening results for the purchaser."

"You didn't know?" Hanson asks, and I shake my head. "That's part of why there are so few TS crimes now. We can trace them far too easily."

I understand that. It makes sense. Somehow, though, part of me still feels angry that someone has Lori's details stored somewhere, complete with a full psych screening. With how important Ink is to her, it seems almost invasive. *Someone's protective*, I taunt myself.

"Okay, so is there any way someone could have gotten hold of the earlier test models?" Hanson asks.

"The models themselves? No. We modified them at each step, as that kept costs lower than if we built multiple different versions. As to the schematics, though? That is, unfortunately, possible."

"Now we're getting somewhere," Hanson says with a smile. "How?"

Hollister opens his hand to me and asks, "When we met before, do you remember what I told you Mr. Redwood intended to do once he'd infiltrated my systems?"

He's referring to Lori's brother, Eddie, whose untimely demise led to my meeting her. "Yeah. He was going to dig up dirt and make it public."

"Quite. When his own system was active on mine, it ran a number of covert tests, one of which was to gather project files and upload them to various unsavoury online sites. We had the postings removed, of course, but it took us a few weeks to catch them all, if indeed we did."

"And one of the postings included the early plans for the TS systems," I conclude with a grimace. "Any number of people could have seen them."

"I am afraid so, yes."

"Whoever viewed the posts could be traced, in theory, but people using the sort of sites I'd guess they were on would have a lot of security to crack if anyone wanted to find them. Not to mention we'd need the URLs of the original posts. Piecing it all together would take a lot of time. That would be fine if we were looking for further corroborating evidence to use in court, but to trace the actual perp?"

Hanson shakes her head and adds her agreement. "Way too long a process. I don't suppose you can think of anyone who would want to put your concepts to nefarious use?"

"Show me a person, and I'll show you someone with the potential for both good and evil," Hollister replies, sadly.

"Ah well, worth a shot." Hanson shrugs. "You recorded this meeting, right?"

"Of course. I'll get a copy sent to you via Captain Hoover. I'll include copies of the reports regarding the postings too."

"Cool. Well, thanks for your time, Mr. Hollister." Hanson rises to her feet and offers a handshake that Hollister reciprocates. I do the same and we head back out to the car.

I pull my seat belt into place and say, "Let's hope Doctor Sanderson found something more useful, eh?"

WE MAKE IT back to the station pretty quickly. Honestly, when I was tearing through the city to escape the Dealer's Sweepers, I didn't really register how the speed I was going felt. I'm gonna guess Lieutenant Hanson got close to it, though it's likely she kept just within the regulated speed limits. If that's true, then I'm glad I was running on auto-pilot to a degree.

"The upper edge of the speed limit is for emergencies only," I comment, reciting an old safety advert from my teen years.

"That and fun," Hanson replies with a chuckle, as she closes her door. "Besides, the good Captain wanted us back quickly. That *is* an emergency. You ever seen him when he's *really* mad? He starts snapping out orders and ends up with a ton of spittle hanging from his moustache. Trust me, as funny as it is that he can go so red, you really don't want to see that. It's goopy."

"It's a good job he likes you."

Hanson shrugs and ushers me through the front door of the station. "Most of the time, he does. He's been on my ass about taking a promotion lately, though, and I think he's getting a little frustrated about my lack of interest."

"Promotion? Wouldn't that put you on the same rank as him?"

"Yup."

"So, what? Is he looking to move up himself?"

Hanson shakes her head. "Not as far as I can tell."

"Which would mean one of you having to move to a new precinct."

"It would. Given how well respected he is, I doubt it would be Captain Hoover who got shifted. That's not why I'm not interested, though."

"No? Then why?"

"I like my workload. I can sink my teeth into the cases I want to, do what I need to, and spend the rest of the time chilling. If I was running a whole station, I wouldn't get a free moment all day." I laugh, and Hanson grins, then continues, "What can I say? We can't all be as work focused as you."

I give her a playful jab in the arm and reply, "I'll have you know, I'm only work focused when I'm actually on a job. The rest of the time, I'm the life of the party."

"T-M-I, Cassie," she says. The accompanying wink is followed by a satisfied grin when she spots me reddening up. She pats me on the shoulder and says, "I'm gonna get into uniform. I'll meet you in the war room."

I nod and go on my way, resisting the urge to try to come up with a smart-ass retort. When I reach the war room, I find that Donal O'Brien, kitted out in a regular police uniform today, is the only other person present. He glances over his shoulder at me when he hears the door shut and pats the water cooler in front of him. "Drink?" he offers.

"Sure," I say, and walk over to take the plastic cup from his hand. "How are you feeling after last night?"

"Angry," he grunts. "This mock paranormal bullshit is beginning to piss me off."

"You saw the shadow people too then, I take it?"

"Yeah. Thought I heard voices too. Have you filed your report yet?"

I nod. "Did it this morning. You?"

"Last night."

I swallow a mouthful of water and make my way to one of the plastic chairs scattered around the centre of the room. "Say, did you notice anything...unexpected about the LV?"

"Other than smashing the lighting not working, ya mean? No. Why's that?"

"I don't know." I sigh. "I could have sworn there was something obvious right in front of me when it attacked, but my brain was so fried by the light show that I couldn't tell what it was. Then, last night, I had this dream. Or a nightmare. The LV was there, but it was female."

Donal chuckles. "Sounds like someone's been reading too many vampire romance novels. Seriously, though, I didn't get any feeling that the LV we fought was a female, if that's what you're getting at."

I snort at myself. "It's stupid."

"Nah, not really." Donal takes the chair next to me. "Sometimes, the subconscious picks up stuff we don't realise. But this time, I think you're barking up the wrong tree."

"Fair enough," I reply. There must have been something else. Something I'm missing. "Hey, I never asked. What rank are you?"

"Does it matter?" he asks, shooting me a curious look.

"Not really, I was just curious. I know Hoove said you're the Marshal of the TS Unit, but I didn't think Marshal was an actual rank here."

"It's not. It works fine as a title, feels like it fits, ya know? But if you want to get technical, I'm a Sergeant. Bec's my supervising Lieutenant."

"Bec?"

"Rebecca. Hanson." Realisation creeps onto my face, and Donal's follows suit. "Ah, feck. She hadn't told you?"

"Nope. I've asked a few times but figured she just doesn't like it or something like that."

"She doesn't. Most people don't know it either, 'cause other than the Captain, no one in the station is high enough ranked to access her files. I think she likes to make a game of it; see who can figure it out, yeah?"

"It's okay, I won't let on." I take another careful sip of water and add, "I'll just save it up in case I want to surprise her."

Donal laughs out loud, and it's a thick, gruff sound. "Ya know, it's a shame you don't work with us more often. I like ya, Cassie. Just don't go doing anything to piss off the wrong person."

And on that ominous note, the door opens and Corporal Devereaux, Captain Hoover, and Doctor Sanderson file in. Hoove moves to the front of the room, looks around and asks, "Where's Lieutenant Hanson?"

"Here," she says, walking in and taking up residence next to Devereaux.

"Okay, good," Hoove says. "First up, Dean Hollister. Anything to report?"

"He said what we saw sounds like one of the early versions of the Boost Jump system, but it was probably taken from the net."

Hoove frowns. "The net?"

"The Redwood case," I clarify. "Whatever Eddie Redwood left on Hollister's systems ran some early tests itself by posting confidential planning files on some dingy little sites, apparently. Hollister volunteered to provide evidence of it, but tracing who downloaded the plans would be a nightmare."

"We'll take that as a closed avenue for now then," Hoove replies. "At least until we check the validity of what he sends us. Okay, in that case, Doctor Sanderson, you're up."

"Yes, of course." The Doctor stands up and moves to the front of the room to join Hoove. The last time I saw him, I was still pretty out of it, but not so much that I shouldn't have noticed at least *something* about the man. Looking at him now, it appears he's just that unremarkable. The jacket he's wearing is a simple lab coat, and it hides his body well. Plain glasses, neatly brushed-back dark hair, and a face placing him in his early forties. That's it.

Sanderson clears his throat and begins, "Mary Warner was, as the file will state, attacked in her home. To reiterate what was said at the hospital, I cannot divulge the nature of the operation she was scheduled for but can assure you it was nothing to worry about. She has been booked in for a long time. If you feel it prudent, you could request the information through official channels, but it would, frankly, be a waste of your time."

"I'll be the one to decide that," Hoove says, an air of impatience tinging his voice. "Get on with it, Doctor."

"Ah, yes. Well. During her X-rays, we found traces of *something* in her arm. Now, I wasn't originally scheduled to carry out her surgery, but I pulled a few strings when she was found to be a victim of our mysterious bloodsucker. This allowed me to remove the fragments that had become embedded under her skin." He reaches into his pocket and pulls out a small plastic pot containing what appears to be a handful of shards of a transparent material.

"Glass," he confirms. "Now, this wouldn't be unusual, under the circumstances. The attacker came in through the window, after all. However, this was strange, as upon closer examination, I found there to be two different types of glass present. One was consistent with most windows these days, but the other...well, it looks far more similar to the glass that was recovered from the scene of Miss Tam's attack."

"So, we think she may have managed to avoid having her blood taken?" Devereaux asks.

Sanderson nods. "It appears likely. I took the liberty of leaving the tracker in place, just in case. As I understand it, the vampire *did* try to sample Miss Tam's blood again, yes?"

"Tried," Donal says. "And failed."

"Well, even if they now give up on that particular sample, it certainly looks like leaving Mrs. Warner's tracker in may prove fruitful."

"Seems that way," Hoove replies. "Has she said anything about the attack yet?"

Sanderson shakes his head. "She arrived unconscious, as I understand it. Under normal circumstances, we would not have gone ahead with her operation, but I felt it could be justified in this instance."

"That's not how hospitals work," Hanson comments.

"No. But falsifying paperwork in extenuating circumstances is. I *did* examine her first to assess the risks."

"You do know that if anything happens to her, at least in relation to the procedure you carried out, I will happily throw you under the bus before I let your methods jeopardise this investigation, don't you?"

Uh oh. From the look on Sanderson's face, he wasn't expecting that response from Hoove. The matter-of-fact way he said it made it even clearer he was serious too. The doctor swallows hard and sputters, "I am *trying* to help the investigation, Captain Hoover, not impede it."

"Just making you aware," Hoove replies and gets to his feet. Sanderson gets out of his way and sits back down, leaving Hoove to stand alone at the front of the room again. "Regardless of the legal ramifications of his methods, I will acknowledge that Doctor Sanderson has presented us with an opportunity here. The two questions we have to ask are one, is a repeat attack likely, and two, how do we take advantage of this?"

"Given the second attempt on me," I tell him, "I'd say there's a good chance of it. What we can do without her consent is going to be an issue, though."

"Agreed," Hanson chimes in. "What are the chances of her waking up any time soon?"

The room goes silent, and all heads turn to Doctor Sanderson. It takes him a moment to realise he's expected to answer. Finally, he says, "Uhm...that is difficult to say. We're not yet sure why she isn't conscious. I have a few blood samples being looked at to try to figure that out. Oh, there are no signs of the proteins in her either."

"Fecking proteins," Donal grumbles.

"Okay," Hanson says, undeterred. "My recommendation is we place the victim under surveillance to see if she wakes up. If it doesn't happen soon, and no attack comes, then we make it less obvious. Hide out in the hospital, and spring a trap."

"Tinted contact lenses will sort the light out," Donal says. "Last night proved that. We still need to figure out what happened after I smashed the fangs, though."

"This gives us some time to work on it," Hanson says and turns to Hoover. "Captain?"

"It's all we've got at the moment. Okay, Corporal Devereaux, you go with Sanderson and take up the first run of surveillance until we can get a proper system in place. The rest of you head out and try to figure out what we're facing here."

"Head out where?" I ask.

"Wherever you think will be useful," Hoove replies, the frustration clear in his voice. "Dismissed."

IN THE END, Donal, Hanson and I decide to convene down in the TS Unit training room to run through a plan of attack.

"I don't like this," Hanson says, hopping up onto a table near the door. "Sanderson's potentially really screwed this up for us."

"I know," Donal grunts. He points at me and says, "Now, you, you're a wily fecker. There was always the chance you'd do something to get away if someone attacked you, but as far as we know, Mary Warner is a regular civilian. Unless she got *real* lucky, she must have spotted something before the attack, or how'd she manage to avoid having her blood taken?"

I shake my head. "I think you're reaching. What you're saying makes sense, but we haven't got anything to back it up. I mean, I still don't know for sure what happened after the LV tried to take my blood."

"Sounded to me like the anonymous caller startled him," Hanson interjects. She shrugs. "He probably panicked and tripped or something. The way the jump boot things work must make them pretty bulky, right? Easy trip hazards right there."

"Maybe," I reply. "How did we hear about Warner?"

"Alarm system tripped when the vamp crashed through the window," Donal says.

"There's your answer," Hanson sighs. "If there was a squad car near enough to the apartment, the sirens could've driven him off before he finished."

Donal nods. "Probably. I still would've liked to have spoken to her before we go much further. I don't like that taking the light show out of the equation didn't stop this guy from fecking me up."

"So, any thoughts on what we do now?" I ask.

"Donal's right," Hanson replies. "We need to prioritise figuring out how else our fanged foe attacks."

"Then...how about you guys work on that, and I'll check out Warner's place?" I ask. Hanson and Donal glance at each other, and I clarify, "I'd have never thought of the Dazzler angle, and I doubt I'll come up with anything else down here. If there's something useful at the house, though, I'll find it."

Donal rubs his stubble thoughtfully and comments, "I guess it's unlikely he'd attack again so soon, even if it *wasn't* daylight. And we *do* need to sort out the contacts if nothing else. Hanson? You have seniority here."

Hanson crosses her arms and considers it for a moment, then says, "Yeah. Yeah, makes sense. Keep in close contact, yeah?"

That last bit was directed at me, so I nod, and wave my goodbyes before heading out the door.

MARY WARNER LIVES on the Western side of the city in an unremarkable house on an unremarkable street. A walk around the outside of the building shows there's nothing out of the ordinary to be found, at least superficially. The house is built like many others, has the same security shutters on the windows. There's no garden, but there *is* a back door that looks as sturdy as the front door. The only damage visible from the outside is the glass window at the back of the building.

"That the shutters weren't down means the attack happened early," I note to myself. "Either that or she's like me and doesn't like pulling the shutters. Good job there isn't an enforced security curfew."

A quick check tells me the doors are locked, so I make my way back around to the broken window and pull out my cell phone. I log into the server for the case and find the official ID file stored in the main folder. With the code displayed on the screen, I hold it up to the scanner by the holographic police tape and wait for the red lights to turn green. They don't. This is a simple system. Each holographic tape line acts as a tripwire. If I cross it without official access being granted, it'll have the same effect as I'm guessing breaking the door in would: it'll summon the cops. Which would be both a pain and a waste of everyone's time in this case. So, I call Hanson.

"Cassie? You found something already?"

"No, I can't get in. The tape is up, but it's not responding to the case clearance on the server."

"Really? Hold on..." I hear some tapping in the background, and Hanson comes back, "Can you read off the code on the side of the projector?"

I lean in, careful to avoid breaking the projection, and say, "A-B-seven-five-P-two-zero-dot-C-C."

"Some idiot typed the second C as a V," Hanson says. "There. It should be working now. If it doesn't, give it five minutes, and try again. If it still doesn't work, call me back, and I'll manually shut it down when you go in."

"Thanks, Hanson," I say, and hang up. I reload the ID and hold it up to the scanner. This time, the lights flash and turn green.

Smiling, I pull myself up and, carefully, climb through the broken window. Inside, there isn't much to see. Sure, there's still some broken glass on the floor, but there are no signs of a struggle in the small kitchen I've climbed into. I load up the official report and skim through it, confirming it was *always* this way, and nobody had done a tidying job. Does that mean Warner didn't hear them smash the window? I guess she could have been listening to music, or sleeping, maybe?

I make my way through an open door to a living room. According to the report, this was where Warner was found, unconscious on the floor. She is the licenced owner of a small handgun, which was found a few feet from her. Looking around, there's no sign of a struggle here either, so it's probably a safe bet that she didn't get to use it. In fact, the only sign of damage is a broken digital picture frame in front of a small table by the stairs. I pull on a pair of gloves—one of the perks of official investigations—and pick up the frame. It's a recent model, which means the screen is pretty tough. If it was simply knocked over, it wouldn't have ended up like this.

I frown. "Two options. Warner must have been upstairs, to begin with, heard the window go, and came down to investigate. Either she tried using the frame as a weapon, then made a grab for the gun afterwards, or the LV broke the frame on purpose. But why would he do that? To make sure she knew he was there, maybe?"

I keep the frame in my hand and head upstairs. There's a modest bathroom at the top of the stairs, a storage cupboard built into one wall, and a bedroom. It's the bedroom I head to, where I find a tidy double bed, a wardrobe, and a desk with a computer on it. One drawer is slightly open. When I glance in, it reveals a spare clip for a handgun. "The gun must have been up here. Warner's gun was near enough to her that it likely spilled out of her hand during the attack, but far enough from the stairs that..." I run through the situation in my head a few times and shake my head. "No, if she'd been disarmed and then gone for the frame, the LV wouldn't have thrown her closer to the gun. *He* must have broken the frame."

The next thing I notice is that the standby light is flashing on the computer's base unit. The screen light is matching it, so I chuck the broken frame onto the bed, give the monitor screen a quick tap, and pull the computer chair out to slip into. A holographic keyboard loads up in front of me, with a big red flashing message reading "Locked."

I look up at the screen, expecting the touchscreen to have the space for a pattern registration, but find myself hit in the face by a red light. I realise too slowly what's happening and push myself away from the desk a little too late. An electronic voice drifts over the speakers, stating, "Retinal Scan complete. Unauthorised access. Please input manual code."

"*Diu,*" I grunt, as the screen loads up the pattern recognition screen I expected, accompanied by a thirty-second timer, creeping its way down towards zero.

*I'm not going to get many shots at this... Everything's tidy. Even the bed is still immaculately made...a tidy shape...*

I swipe my hand over the touchscreen monitor, trying a square, but it tells me that this is incorrect.

*What did that article last week say was the most common one? A spiral?*

It isn't a spiral either.

The countdown reaches zero, and the screen goes dead. Next, there's a pop, and the base unit starts to smoke. I slap my forehead. It won't be a fire hazard, but this is a fairly popular security system these days. The computer is now fried. Great.

Frustrated, not to mention slightly embarrassed I didn't notice the clear retinal scanner on the top of the monitor, I pull out another drawer on the desk and start rifling through the contents. I spread the neatly filed papers over the bed. Most of them are print copies of bills. Right in the middle is a tenancy agreement that shows Mary Warner's moving-in date as being a little over a week ago. Her previous address, as shown on the accompanying letter, is...in California?

"Didn't Sanderson say she'd been booked in for her surgery for a long time? I guess it could have been a specialist thing and she moved here to make it easier to access? No, that doesn't make sense. If it was a specialist surgery, she wouldn't want the stress of moving first. Or would that be *less* stress, knowing she was near home? Let's see what else we have."

I pull out another wad of papers and find an official visiting slip for the New Hopeland Prison, dated a few days ago. Now, who was she visiting...? "Malcolm Castleford?"

I drop the paper on the pile and frown, bringing my fist up to my face. *Why would she be visiting* him?

My eyes stray to the broken picture frame. The report didn't mention a check on the computer, probably because the cops on hand wouldn't have known about the LVs so wouldn't have been looking at anything other than the room the attack took place in. That would have been left for the eventual investigating officer. But it didn't mention the frame being checked either.

I fumble through the drawers, find a cable that will fit it, and hook it up to my phone. A quick browse shows there's only one file on it, a single photo, so I copy it over and unhook the device. A few quick taps later and I'm greeted with a shot of three people, a man, a woman, and a child, gathered around a table in a restaurant. I pinch zoom and study the faces in the photo. The woman looks a little like the shot we have on file for Mary Warner, but younger. The man is strangely familiar. There's something about his facial structure that's registering, but I can't place a name. And the child...

*That's Allen Fuerza.*

# Chapter Six

THE NEW HOPELAND prison is situated several miles outside the city. It *should* be a pain to get to, all things considered, but thanks to a Government funded initiative, several cab firms are always open to pick you up from the North West city exit and shuttle you there and back. You just have to let the driver flash your barcoded visitor papers at the start of each part of the trip. That allows the Government computers to register the GPS position of the cab and confirms the trip is official, making it easy to match up funds for transfer.

As to why the Government would want to fund travel for prison visitors? I always wondered about that myself, and I only found out the reason by accident. Lori and I were chatting one evening about two weeks ago, and the subject of New Hopeland's legal eccentricities came up. It's a minefield in a way, given the relationship between her brother's death and Devin Carmichael, but there are some really odd little things in New Hopeland that make for good conversation pieces. I happened to mention the cab shuttle service and Lori told me a story. It turns out that the news photos she takes don't always fall on the right side of the law. There had been rumours of a large number of Government officials visiting the prison, and not always to see family and friends who had made some unfortunate life choices. That wouldn't have been a big issue if said officials hadn't been claiming the trips as *Government business* for years and writing them off as expense claims.

The IRS started getting suspicious and, being the big scary lot they are, commenced an investigation, which tipped off the news sites to there being something worth prying into. So, a single reporter and his photographer did some snooping during an office tour and turned up a number of files that were in the process of being edited to show legitimate travel claims. Now, the owner of the news site happened to have a few members of staff behind bars and came up with a plan. She protected both Lori and her paired reporter's identity, of course, and let the Government know in no uncertain terms what she was going to release to both the public *and* the IRS, unless they rushed something through for her: the prison travel scheme.

The officials involved saw the positives of the idea, the main one being that their fraudulent claims would be lost in the sands of time, and went ahead with the initiative. Lori sees the benefits for the public, as well as for her job, but still kinda feels that the fraud should have been revealed. But that's New Hopeland for you. The main thing from my standpoint is that getting to the prison when I need to has become a lot easier, and a lot cheaper, at least as long as I stay within the monthly visit limits. For today's visit, working with the PD also helped, as it meant I could get an order for visitation rushed to my phone to allow me to make use of the scheme.

The trip was pleasant enough. The roads are well maintained because, well, that's what happens when those with the power to affect such things are themselves making use of the thing they can affect. On top of that, even during standard hours, the roads never quite hit the point of being congested. Most people know *someone* in prison these days, but not everyone wants to visit them at all, let alone often. In fact, I wouldn't be surprised if the primary users of the prison visitation scheme are the ones who barely escaped the tax authorities. We arrive ahead of time and my relatively quiet driver is happy to sit back with a baseball game streaming onto his tablet while I do what I need to.

Getting in early isn't a problem either, as it turns out. "Prisoner MC6C30," the guard who leads me through the winding halls explains, "is under strict supervision right now. That was why we allowed the request for a private room."

"Makes him easier to watch than if he's in the public space," I reply, following my guide into the elevator. "So, what did he do to warrant the extra security?"

The guard hits the button for floor C and sniffs uncomfortably. "I am not at liberty to say, regardless of your position. I'm sure it will all become clear when you see him, however."

I nod. "Fair enough. Does he know who's coming to talk to him?"

"He does. Can't say he seemed like he was expecting you, though."

"No. He wouldn't be."

The elevator comes to a stop and we step out into another overly sanitised hallway. We only make it two steps before the guard places a hand on my shoulder and leans in to say, "I shouldn't be telling you this, but keep your eyes open. The moment he heard you were visiting, he made a phone call and arranged a second visitor. He isn't the sort who we can stop visiting, so expect him to join you at some point."

I steel myself and reply, "Noted. How long will I likely have to get what I need before I'm interrupted?"

"I wish I knew. This way," he says and starts heading down to a door at the far end of the hallway.

*Well, isn't that wonderful,* I grumble to myself. *Fingers crossed whoever he called is a Fuerza goon who knows what I know and isn't about to hold it against me.*

I step into a small room containing a single table and two chairs but wait until the door is closed to step forward. The guard wasn't kidding. Looking at Malcolm Castleford right now, it's not difficult to figure out why he's being watched. Even with the orange prison uniform on, it's easy to see that he's lost weight since I last saw him. The black eye and the stitches on the side of his head give away a lot more than weight loss, though.

"Someone's not been playing nice," I say, pulling out a chair.

"Spare me, Detective," he grunts. "To what do I owe the pleasure?"

"I'm doing great, thanks for asking." I shoot him a sarcastic grin. Then remember I'm time limited here. "I'm working a case with the PD."

"Yes, yes, alongside Donal O'Brien no doubt. I know about..." And just like that, he shuts his mouth and pulls down a far sterner mask for himself. "I hear things. Rumours. Let's leave it at that. Given what you're likely investigating, I fail to see why you need to speak with *me*, Detective."

"Okay, then let's get straight to the point." I glance over my shoulder to make sure the guard isn't watching too closely through the glass in the door and sneak my cell phone out. I load up the picture I found at Mary Warner's house. I show Castleford and he does a decent job of feigning ignorance. But there was enough of a twitch in one eye for me to know that he knows who we're looking at. "Who is that in the photo, Castleford?"

"How would I know?" he tries, sitting back.

"Because the woman, Mary Warner, visited you a few days ago. She's in a coma, by the way. Or that's how it sounds to me anyway. Tell me, what did you two talk about?"

"Nothing I can tell you about."

"Try again."

"I am serious, Detective. Tell me, was she attacked by...the *person* you're trying to track down with the police?"

"Trade. One answer for another."

Castleford groans loudly and slaps his hands on the table. "Fine. We were discussing Allen Fuerza, if you must know. Now, was she attacked?"

"Yes. And yes, it was likely by the person we're tracking, as you put it. The photo, Castleford. I recognised Warner, and the child is Fuerza. Who's the man?"

"You're the detective. You figure it out."

"I know we don't see eye to eye, but if Mary Warner was visiting you, then you either like her or you can see a use for her. If you won't help me, then help me help her."

"Help you? I already have."

"How the hell have you helped me, Castleford?"

He groans again and grumbles, "This is all so confusing. I don't know what to tell you, Tam. Or to be more precise, I don't know what I'm *allowed* to tell you. This," he says, waving his cuffed hands at his facial injuries, "is nothing compared to what will happen if I screw this up."

I sigh. "Then *think*. What have I already pretty much figured out, but not confirmed? You should be able to tell me that without getting in trouble, eh? I already know it, sort of."

Castleford blinks and turns his head away. I can see from the look in his eyes that he's considering my words carefully. Finally, he says, "Mary Warner has known Allen

Fuerza for a very long time. While this *does* involve him, it's not in the way you'd expect. You see, she knows his real name, but not *who* he is."

"Okay, good. I *did* already know that he isn't to blame for this."

"Isn't he?" Castleford laughs. "Just because he didn't order it, doesn't mean he's not responsible, Detective. How much of what happens in New Hopeland can be attributed to him indirectly, I wonder? I will tell you this, though; if I had succeeded last month, none of what you're dealing with right now would have happened."

I start to respond, but the door opens, and Castleford turns his head towards our visitor. "Todd Eyre, as you thought. I said nothing."

"And has he been able to inform the target?" the visitor asks, and I don't even need to turn around to know who it is.

"The detective will be able to confirm that. Hence my calling you," Castleford replies, then yells, "I'm ready to go back to my cell now."

The guard from earlier enters, and a second guard comes with him. The new arrival takes Castleford by the cuffs and leads him from the room, leaving my original escort to say, "Follow me, please."

I rise and walk silently on one side of the guard, with the ever eerily calm Sunglasses Paloma on the other side. The elevator ride is equally as silent until we hit the ground floor. Sunglasses walks out, but the guard stops me and whispers, "Everything okay?"

I keep my face stony, but reply, "Yeah. Thanks," and walk out of the building, watching as the Four Kings of Utah's number one problem solver makes his way to the only car in the public lot that isn't my cab. When his car doesn't move, I walk over to my cab, give the window a tap, and say to the driver, "I'll be back in ten minutes."

The cab driver waves me on nonchalantly and I make my way to Sunglasses' shiny black Mercedes. I open the passenger side door and slide in. He relaxes in his seat and says, "It is good to see you again, Miss Tam."

"I wish I could say the feeling's mutual."

He nods, and asks, "I assume something has happened to Miss Warner?"

I sigh. "It's not like you won't find out, anyway. She was attacked by the Light Vampire. You know about him, eh?"

"Yes. We do not yet know *who* he is, but we are aware of his existence."

"Then how about you throw a dog a bone here? What's the link between Mary Warner, Malcolm Castleford, and Allen Fuerza?"

Sunglasses turns his head towards me. "You understand that what little I can tell you is of no use to your investigation, do you not?"

"Sure. But if it gives me something I can piece together another way, it may still give me a way to bring this to a close."

"I see. If you are asking me about a link between the three then perhaps you could share what you *do* know already?"

I nod and pull out my cell phone to show him the photo. "I know Mary Warner knew Allen Fuerza when he was a child, and Castleford confirmed she knows his real name, but not who he really is. I also know she visited Castleford at least once, a few days ago."

"She is a long-time acquaintance of the di Franco family. The file you have is from an old news article. A reverse picture search will tell you who the man in the photo is and how she knows him. As to her visiting Castleford, that began as an accident. She happened to be on site with a now ex-colleague of hers from California, and recognised Mr. Fuerza when he left a meeting with Mr. Castleford."

"And was his visit to Castleford linked to all of this?"

"In a way. It was common knowledge that Mr. Castleford had upset the Kings, and someone had been pressing him for information regarding the identity of the King's Guard. When Miss Warner reached out through Castleford, we were...wary. There was undoubtedly an opportunity to move certain plans forward, however, and so we fed her some information."

"The names of King's Guard members."

"Yes. Not all of them, of course, only those we believed would be able to take the correct approach to what would ensue. We knew the Light Vampire would be visiting, but not what he would do."

"Not all of the victims are King's Guard. Are the rest of us random attacks?"

"I cannot be certain in most cases, but *you* were certainly not random."

Something clicks into place, and I growl, "You told her I was King's Guard."

"I am afraid so. We were aware of the legal issues that were about to befall you and, having ascertained how the Light Vampire worked by this point, fed your name out to him through Miss Warner. It was a calculated risk, but we believed, given the correct assistance, this would ensure you did not serve jail time. Had Captain Hoover not come up with the idea of inviting you onto the investigation, Mr. O'Brien was under orders to push the idea himself."

"Not that I don't appreciate the thought, but I don't like being thrown into this without being warned first. Why me?"

"Because you understand the rules, Miss Tam. Even with the trappings of an official investigation to stifle you, you are still pursuing your own path, as we knew you would. The fact remains that some people are more useful when incarcerated. *You* are more useful when able to move freely."

"So, what? I'm a problem solver for Allen Fuerza now?"

"Only in certain circumstances."

My hand balls into a fist. "And was the anonymous caller who sent the police my way planned?"

"Yes. I ensured that the LV did not take his sample and made the call myself. To my knowledge, he likely believes me to be Mr. Farrah."

"Well thanks for that," I say through gritted teeth. "Okay, so how does this Todd Eyre fit into all of this?"

"He belonged to Brett Stantz but was unhappy with being made a sacrificial lamb. It was my belief that he would be problematic, and he has now proven himself so."

I frown. "He beat Castleford, didn't he?" Sunglasses nods, and I continue, "He must have overheard him giving out King's Guard names. But if he's proven himself to be... He overheard something he shouldn't have, and reported to whoever Mary Warner and the Light Vamp is working for... How much is this reverse picture search going to help me?"

"If you follow the breadcrumbs as you normally do, it will give you enough. Your task will be to find a way to piece it together without revealing anything unfortunate. And that, I am afraid, is all I can say at this point. I do have one question for you, if you would indulge me, however."

"You may as well."

"Is Miss Warner still alive?"

"Yeah."

"That *is* surprising. Perhaps you may wish to consider why it may be."

I grunt a thanks, or as close as I'm willing to give, and exit the car. I hear the engine start up before I even make it back to my cab. When I get in, the driver is smiling happily at his game. He glances up at me and, with a concerned look on his face, asks, "Is everything okay?"

"It better fucking end up that way."


THE CAB DRIVER takes my mood as a prompt to drive silently, concentrating on the audio commentary for the continuing game. That's useful as it gives me a chance to run the reverse picture search on my cell phone. There are a few hits, all on news sites. While the wording varies a little from site to site, the general message remains the same, and I'm able to piece a timeline of events together.

Twenty-five years ago, Mary Warner was known as Pauline Welch. She was suspected of several crimes, ranging from delivery of illicit goods to murder. All these crimes had links to Angel Tanner, the owner of a California *business* specialising in gun running and drug dealing. Though she was questioned on multiple occasions, the California PD were never able to make anything stick, and she flat-out refused to sell out Tanner. This particular picture was taken alongside Arthur di Franco and his then nine-year-old son, Casille.

The significance of the photo is twofold. First, Arthur was instrumental in ensuring Pauline was not sent to prison, providing watertight alibis for her on multiple occasions. Second, it was taken less than one week before the crime that *did* finally see her do jail time: the murder of Arthur di Franco.

The facts of the case were fairly straightforward. Pauline was found at the scene of the crime, the murder weapon in hand, and admitted to killing di Franco the moment the cops arrived. The boy was nowhere to be found, and Pauline was adamant he must have run away when he heard the gunshots. Whether her story is true or not is anyone's guess, but I do know that Casille resurfaced later on as the author of *Four Steps To Power*, and then disappeared again to become Allen Fuerza.

Regardless, the news sites soon forgot about Casille; he was just another child of a criminal, caught up in a criminal dispute, and would be no loss to anyone. The court case was open and shut, with Pauline pleading guilty and receiving a sentence of fifteen years. The story she told was that Arthur had been caught doing something he shouldn't, and when she had tried to talk him out of it, he became aggressive and she was forced to defend herself. The official word was that he was dealing drugs that didn't fit with the modern criteria for things-the-police-can-let-slide, and this was backed up by a stash of cocaine in his residence.

The interesting thing is several members of the conspiracy crowd picked up the story, and their tale was a little different. The general consensus seemed to be that Arthur had indeed been doing something he shouldn't: working with a law enforcement agency to bring down Angel Tanner. He had allegedly been caught red-handed by Angel herself, and it was said that it was she who pulled the trigger. Believing Pauline to potentially be working with the now deceased Arthur di Franco, Angel gave her the opportunity to prove herself by taking the rap for the murder.

Casille di Franco really had disappeared before anything could happen to him, though nobody really seems to know how or why. That didn't bother Angel. As long as

Pauline maintained her guilt, it wouldn't even matter if the boy later turned up and said he'd seen something different.

The theory allegedly came from a nameless source in the prison that held Pauline. She was let out after serving ten years, and immediately returned to Angel's side. Searching her name shows she then spent several years in pretty much the same position as she had previously: she was suspected of various crimes but had alibis that prevented her from being locked up again. It's when I'm scrolling through her most recent news appearances that I spot something interesting. Another photo, this time far closer in appearance to the one we have on file. This shows Pauline Welch standing alongside the man who had provided *irrefutable proof* she had not been present at the scene of a multiple homicide, one that had strangely involved the victims being drained of much of their blood. That man was Doctor Harold Sanderson.

*Now I just have to figure out what I can tell the rest of the team without revealing something* unfortunate.


IN THE END, I decided I couldn't mention Sunglasses or what he'd told me about Fuerza being involved in the leak of names. Instead, I claimed Castleford had leaked some names to Welch—or Warner now—because he felt aggrieved by the whole mess last month. I'm pretty sure Donal will make sure he gets the message to play up on that if asked. The picture stuff was easy enough to spin off from there as a natural next step.

"Dev's gonna need to be caught up on all of this," Hanson says after I finish explaining what I'd turned up.

Captain Hoover snorts and starts tapping away at his keyboard. "Damn right he is. Let's see if we can find anything in the California database that'll help tie this together. What date was the multiple homicide?"

I check my cell again and confirm, "Sometime in June two years ago."

"Okay..." Hoove grunts, his eyes scanning the cases in front of him. "Okay, here we go. All surveillance equipment cut before attack...no prints, no survivors... They originally tried pinning it on Pauline Welch as she was spotted nearby and has a history of aggressive behaviour, though this has only led to one conviction... It says here that the case remains open in terms of identifying the assailant with any certainty. With no witnesses, living or mechanical, not to mention no similar or potentially related events happening prior to the attack, they had no real leads on an assailant. As an interesting addendum, a large delivery of blood was made to the hospital shortly after, with the types matching those of the victims. Due to a combination of incomplete medical files and the cremation of the bodies, DNA testing was only able to identify two of the seven victims in the delivery. There was no record of who ordered or supplied the blood, and it was only found by chance when an industrious receptionist decided to double-check the records before moving it to the relevant storage area."

"If we're dealing with the same person here, we could be looking at an underground blood trade," I say. "There's been a big drop in donors over the last few years, and the synthesised stuff has a high rate of rejection right now, doesn't it?"

"It would make sense," Donal replies. "Maybe that case was too close for comfort for the perp, and they're taking it more slowly this time. Relocate to a new city and sample a bunch of people, then when the need arises, they can check for blood type matches to source fluid for delivery."

"If they're sampling on that basis, they may be going deeper than type when it comes to selection," Hanson adds. "They could be looking at getting as close a match as possible from the standpoint of genetic defects or strengths too. I read that there's a lot of research being done into taking closer matches where possible. It's something to do with responsiveness to medication that needs to be taken at the same time for other issues."

"Still, seven victims at once. Any chance our LV could have pulled that off?" Hoove asks and glances towards Donal.

The Irishman rubs his chin thoughtfully and replies, "Depends on the victims and the circumstances. If he took them one by one, and did it quietly, maybe. The news report said they were all in the same room, though, right?" I nod, and he continues, "It was two years ago. The tech could have changed a lot over that time. His gear could have been built more for multiple encounters back then."

"Sounds to me like you're just trying to get it to fit," Hoove says, his upper lip twitching and crinkling his moustache.

"The number forty-eight," I say, my eyes going wide. "Could there really be that many?"

"Thus far, it seems like there's only one here," Hanson replies. "But we can't rule out there being more. Not now."

Hoove sighs and sits back into his chair. "I'm open to suggestions as to how we deal with this. For one, we need to figure out whether to try to pump the esteemed Mr. Castleford for more information."

I shake my head. "I wouldn't. Not yet anyway. He was pretty beat up when I spoke to him, so he's obviously been upsetting the wrong people already. Even if we take him aside for a private meeting, the other prisoners will likely know. If it were me running the case on my own, I'd leave him alone unless it became absolutely necessary. Given the professional links here, though, it may be worth getting some of the guards to keep an eye on things."

"They probably are already," Donal comments. "I can check it. I've got some buddies on that side of things, and I'm sure they'd be happy to make sure he stays alive long enough to testify if needed."

Hoove's eyes slide over to Lieutenant Hanson, who appears to now be fiddling with her cell phone. His brow furrows into an angry grimace, and he growls, "Not boring you, are we, Lieutenant?"

"Not at all," Hanson replies, keeping her own gaze on her phone screen.

"Then perhaps you'd like to share your thoughts on what we're discussing?"

"You know me, Cap. I love a good interrogation, and I'd normally have no problem hauling Castleford across the coals again. But in this case, I think Cassie is right."

"Why's that? And put your fucking phone down."

Hanson smiles, pulling every ounce of innocence she can onto her face, and gets to her feet. She struts across the room and hands her phone to Hoove, stating simply, "That's why."

Hoove starts scrolling through something, his lips moving slightly as he reads silently to himself. I can tell this is bad, because he isn't making any move to remove Hanson from her new position sitting on the edge of his desk, kicking her legs idly. Once he's finished, he hands the phone back to Hanson and shoos her from the desk. "As Lieutenant Hanson has just shown me, Angel Tanner has been making some noise down in California about challenging the Four Kings of Utah. That would tie up with the attacks on those known to be linked with the Kings appearing to be pre-planned. I think we better come up with a way to end this sooner rather than later. I *do not* want New Hopeland turning into an inter-state gang war zone. O'Brien, did you make any headway on the contact lenses?"

"They should be ready to pick up by now. We'll need to test them, though. And figure out what else the LV—or LVs—are doing."

"Okay. You go grab the lenses now and bring them back here. Any thoughts on the other trick?"

"Bert's in for repairs," I reply. "They're gonna check through his data logs to check if there's any indication of why he attacked like he did. That *could* give us some idea of what happened."

"In that case, get on to the repair team and see if they've got anything for us. If you need to visit them directly, I'll get you an escort. Bert wasn't affected by the LV, so if he's battle-ready, he'd potentially be a good addition if you're fine with that?" I nod, and Hoove continues, "Hanson, give Devereaux a call and explain what we're dealing with. Make sure he knows not to give anything away to anyone, but especially Doctor Sanderson. Have him stay there to guard the victim but tell him to be careful. Once your jobs are done, we'll reconvene here so that we can hammer out a plan."

And so, for the second time today, we all file out of the war room mand start heading our own way. Hoove, no doubt responsible for multiple operations right now, makes a beeline back up the hall towards the stairs to his office. Hanson follows along, though she'll detour to her desk to call Corporal Devereaux. Donal waits back a little and beckons me over to the ramp down to the TS area.

"Good job in there," he says, after checking we're alone. "I'll get Castleford caught up on what he needs to say if anyone pays him a visit. Was it only him you spoke to?"

I shake my head. "Nah, another King's Guard turned up. Big guy in a suit, shaven head, neat beard, dark skin. Sunglasses Paloma I call him."

Donal laughs. "You have *him* down as a Paloma?"

"The first time I met him was during the Castleford case. He was masquerading as a Paloma then."

"The poor sod. Sunglasses, though... You don't do well with getting people's names, do you?"

"I get them when they're freely given. Not everyone likes to give them out. Or in some cases, not their real names."

"Aye, true enough. In that case, good job on not bringing him into it either."

I shrug. "Seemed safer if we're trying to keep Allen Fuerza away from the spotlight."

Donal gives me a slap on the shoulder. It'd annoy me if a member of the public did it, but it's a common thing among members of the PD, so I let it slide as a sign that I'm an accepted member of the team. "Good lass," he says. "So, are ya heading out to FE Limited, or are you gonna call them?"

"I'll call ahead, but I'm hoping I can drop in. If Bert's ready, or will be soon, I can pick him up that way."

Donal nods and says, "Well, in that case, I'll see ya back here in a bit," and heads back up the hallway towards the main station.


I DIDN'T ENTIRELY lie to Donal. The ability to pick Bert up did form part of my decision to head over to the Familiar

Enterprises offices. Truth be told, my paranoia engine is beginning to warm up. The way this case is going, it's going to be difficult to keep it all in check. Given he's no doubt more experienced with the cover-up side of things, I'm glad Donal is on board with this, but I'm getting the distinct impression that I need to be careful with who's listening to what right now. That being the case, I'd rather get a private room to talk to Doctor Faraday. Sure, FE Ltd are no doubt controlling things within their building, and I wouldn't be surprised if the conversation was recorded for their *testing*, but as long as I'm careful with what I say, I'm confident the conversation will go no further by *their* hand.

After an awkwardly quiet journey with a chaperone who, not knowing what I'm working on, obviously feels like his time is being wasted, I make my way into the building. The check-in process is nice and quick, and I head straight up to today's home away from home, the third floor. Brenda is back at the desk again and does the honours of taking me to Doctor Faraday. The human-shaped familiar regards me with a curious look and waves Brenda away so that we can speak in private.

"Hello, Doctor Faraday. Thank you for seeing me on such short notice."

"I noted that you called from a number registered to the police station. Given you're likely working on this case of yours, I thought it prudent to offer assistance."

I nod in agreement and ask, "How's Bert doing?"

"Straight to the point. Good. I loathe small talk at the best of times. Too many openings to slip up. Though I suppose that doesn't matter with you. Regardless, he will be fine. The initial examination showed only superficial damage to his outer shell, but upon closer inspection, it *does* appear there are some near misses internally. In layman's terms, this means his chassis has been compromised and any direct impact would likely result in his internal systems becoming damaged. As such, the repairs will take a little longer than I had originally anticipated."

"Ah. How long do you think he'll be out of action?"

"Bert is classed as a priority case, so you can expect him back within the next three days."

"That...he would have been really useful right now."

"Well, a quicker repair is certainly possible, but he would need to be returned to us as soon as possible after the cessation of whatever you need him for so that we could finish the job."

"What would the risks be?"

"As already stated, if he were to suffer a direct impact to the affected areas, his internal systems would be damaged. That would mean a far longer repair job, and most likely a full reset of anything we can't back up. Depending on your viewpoint of AI technology, this could be seen as a death for him. Or part of him, certainly."

"Death..." I repeat, mulling her words over in my head. "I've never really considered death in relation to Bert before."

"I see. Then am I to take it that you have not truly viewed him as on par with a living being of flesh and blood?"

"That's complicated... I haven't really sat down and acknowledged it, but... I haven't ever looked at him as just a machine either. I mean, I know he *is* a machine on a base level, but he has his own little personality, eh? He's...he's unique. I don't know if I'd even fully consider him a pet at this point."

"Is he more or less than a pet to you?"

I pause and think about it for a moment, then answer firmly, "More. He's both a guard dog and house pet, yes, but he's there in the same way as a close friend sometimes. Or as much as he can be, anyway."

"Fascinating. Should I proceed with a temporary fix for Bert, or are you happy to wait for the full maintenance?"

"Take as long as you need. I wouldn't want any part of him to die. Did you have the chance to go through his behaviour and memory logs yet?"

"We have. Would you like a summary of the points of interest?"

"Please."

"Running through the evening he took the damage, he saw something watching your apartment. I say *something* as he has catalogued the being as both hostile and a monster rather than as a human or animal. They were not visible by normal optical scans, though they did show up on thermal. He would not even have checked this setting if it had not been that he happened to pick up a pulsing auditory disturbance aimed at your *sleep quarters*."

"An auditory disturbance?"

"Yes. He continued to track the disturbance when you left the building and confirmed that it was following you. He did not act initially as he believed your body language to be such that you were aware of its presence. He was also aware of a companion who would offer some protection for you. From the detail in his internal visualisation, I would assume it was the Tech Shifter you mentioned before. Even so, he knew you were likely in danger and eventually made the decision to act. He did not want to go through the window as, although it was a quicker route, he knows you prefer him not to damage the apartment. He calculated a minimum time needed to intervene, however, and would have broken out through the window anyway if the door had not been opened for him.

"Tracking you down was easy due to the link on your cell phone, and when he arrived, both you and your companion were already suffering. He decided this was likely due to the auditory disturbance, which he registered as having increased in level, and so he targeted the source of this."

"Did he register any details about the audio? I couldn't hear anything specific."

"He did not. Bert's programming is such that, while he technically *could* ascertain such things given time, he is more likely to act quickly if he believes it to be in your best interests. For what it is worth, he does so as he is *happy* to have found a home with you. Whether this is true happiness or a simulated response, I will leave up to you to decide."

"Okay. Okay, that's a good start for us."

"That he registered the attacker as a monster was interesting. I must confess, Miss Tam, I am a little curious."

"If I could tell you more, then I would. As it stands, it's all confidential. Maybe once the case is closed, I'll be able to, though it'll probably be nothing more than gets released publicly."

"I understand. I am what you would call a fan of the more unusual news sites online, and simply wished to clarify if the attacker had anything to do with the rumoured genetic mutation research that has been doing the rounds with the conspiracy theorists of late."

"I hadn't seen any of that. I can confirm we're not dealing with a genetic mutant, though. The monster thing is probably due to my own reaction. It's definitely a straight-up human, just one who came prepared for a particular task."

"I see. Well, I thank you for that information, at least. Was there anything else?"

"No, that'll be it for now. Thank you, Doctor Faraday."

"You are welcome, Miss Tam. I shall be in touch once Bert is ready."

I exit the building as quickly as I entered it because, well, I don't want to leave a bad taste in my escort's mouth. His continuing to give me the silent treatment is useful, though, as it gives me a chance to think through what I've learned. By the time we're back at the station, I have an idea. Or I have two words anyway. Confident they may help, I march straight up to Lieutenant Hanson's desk and slam my hands down in front of her. She glances up at me and, in a move that probably makes me look like I've lost my mind, I smile and say, "Dog whistles."

"SO," HOOVE SAYS, pacing in front of his desk in the war room, "you're telling me you had a dream about an LV winding some dogs up, is that right?"

"Yeah."

"And that combined with the report of Bert tracking an auditory disturbance makes you think our perp is using a dog whistle in conjunction with the lighting?"

"Yeah. Or something similar, anyway."

When Hoove speaks again, his voice is firm, though not aggressive. "The problem is that dog whistles don't generally affect humans much at all unless they have an underlying condition."

"I know that," I reply. "But the concept could be similar."

"Actually," Hanson cuts in, "Cassie could be onto something here. You ever hear of Vic Tandy?"

"Who?" Hoove asks.

"He was a British engineer," Hanson clarifies. "He was a pioneer in the use of infrasound in paranormal research. See, he was working in some lab, and he kept getting this...feeling of fear, I guess. He said he saw some sort of apparition too, but every time he tried to look directly at it, it disappeared."

Hoove sighs and sits down into his chair. "And what does this have to do with dog whistles, exactly?"

"Well, this Tandy guy figured out there was something in the lab—a fan I think it was—vibrating at a frequency a little below nineteen Hz. When he turned it off, all the anxiety dropped off, and his apparition disappeared. It's why some people call the eighteen-point-nine Hz range 'the fear frequency.' Dog whistles, now they go a little above twenty Hz, which is why you can't hear them; twenty Hz is the upper limit for most humans."

"Then why'd I get the idea of dog whistles in my head?" I ask.

"New Hopeland isn't exactly a silent city, right? You'd have likely heard anything the LV was putting out below twenty Hz, but it would have been like the sort of ambient noise that surrounds you every day."

"So, it wouldn't have registered with me what I was hearing."

"And the same with me," Donal cuts in from the doorway. "Sound below twenty Hz," he says and waves Hanson to continue.

"Exactly. Now, I'm no psychiatrist..."

"Thank fuck for that," Hoove cuts in, then looks slightly embarrassed that he's spoken out loud. "Sorry. Continue."

Hanson gives the Captain a wink then turns to me and says, "Something in you must have picked up on it being odd and your brain went to the first thing that seemed familiar and similar. Dog whistles."

"That would make sense," I reply. "What sort of response does the fear frequency get in people?"

"Aside from anxiety and hallucinations, it varies. Dizziness, terror, confusion, that sort of thing. Then there's the brown note."

"Which might explain the nightmare too. Wait...the brown note?" I ask.

"Yeah, if a note goes low enough, you stop being able to hear it, and the theory is if you find the right frequency, you can make someone shit their—"

"Thank you, Lieutenant Hanson," Hoove says, stopping her a little too late for my liking. "Assuming we're right about this, is there a reason why the LV wouldn't be using the auditory tactic all the time?"

"Inconsistency," Hanson replies. "The results vary a lot from person to person, and it's actually even less consistent than the dazzler lights. My guess is he uses it as a sort of backing track to the attack, then switches it to the primary weapon as a last resort. From there, he probably varies up the frequency until he gets a response."

"Testing the theory would be ideal," Hoove grunts, "but it's at least an easy one to solve. We have noise cancelling headphones on site." He turns to Donal and asks, "Are the lenses ready?"

"Got 'em down in the TS area ready for us to test."

AS IT TURNS out, I find contact lenses uncomfortable. Not that we have much choice in the matter right now. I'd say they're less conspicuous than sunglasses, but with the odd-coloured tinting, these things stand out. A lot.

Hanson flashes a few more lights in my face, and much like the last two tests, they have no effect on me. I turn to

Donal and say, "It's great that they work, but they're a solid brown. Don't you think it's going to be obvious?"

Donal shrugs. "Sure it is, but that's the tinting for you. The LV already knows we found a way around his little light show anyway, so even if there *is* more than one of them, he'll have passed that little titbit on."

"I guess, but what about the public? However we tackle this, we're likely to see regular people at some point. Isn't it going to look a bit odd?"

"Self-conscious?" he asks with a smirk. I flip the bird his way, and he smiles, then continues, "We can work around it. We'll say it's a charity thing or something."

"Your eye guard is clear," I remind him.

"It's made from a different material. And by a different person. Does the tinting obscure your vision?"

"No."

"Then there's no problem. It only shows up in strong light anyway."

"Do Corporal Devereaux's work?" Hoove asks.

"No way to tell for sure without testing them," Donal replies.

"Seems like a good bet given the rest all work," Hanson adds. "I doubt he'd want us wearing them for him anyway. He can get a bit weird with germs sometimes."

"We'll risk it then. Just make sure he knows his aren't tested," Hoove says.

"Great. So, any ideas on how to proceed?" Hanson asks.

"I've been thinking about that," Hoove says. "I say we tackle this head on."

"And how do we do that?"

"We alone down here?" Hoove asks, and Donal nods. "We know for certain who Mary Warner is, and we have a good idea who the LV is, we just need the proof. So, let's make him panic. We're going to throw out a direct challenge for tonight and force his hand."

# Chapter Seven

CAPTAIN HOOVER STANDS behind the podium we've set up in the war room and waits for the noise from the assorted people we've invited to die down before looking right at the camera and starting his pre-prepared speech. "Ladies and gentlemen, I am sure you are aware of the recent increase in crime in the city, in particular as it pertains to muggings. While many of these crimes are unrelated to one another, other than in their general nature, a great number can be attributed to one individual. Until now, we have remained silent on this, but the time has come to confirm that the attacker in question is not targeting individuals in order to steal material possessions. He, and we are certain it is a *he*, has been stealing small samples of the victims' blood."

The gathered reporters start to shout out questions, mostly along the lines we expected going into this. Hoove silences them with his hands and responds, "I am sure you can understand that our overall aim was to reduce the risk of causing panic among the general public. Yes, our intent has always been to reveal the details of the case, but not until we were in a position to ensure public safety. Since the beginning of the attacks, a small team of our finest has been tackling the case and, more recently, we were fortunate enough to be able to bring in additional help from outside the department. I am sure that, given her recent involvement with a number of high-profile cases in the city, you all know Cassandra Tam. I would like to hand the microphone to her now to deliver an important message to those watching, and to one person in particular."

I shake Hoove's hand before replacing him behind the podium. Once the initial murmur has subsided, I say, "Thank you, Captain Hoover, for both the kind words and the opportunity to play my part in resolving this matter. Most of you know me already, but for those who don't, I am a licenced private investigator here in New Hopeland and have been now for many years. I am sure you are all wondering why the PD have contracted someone such as myself onto their team, especially given the disparity between resources available to each of us. The reason is simple. Recently, I almost became a victim of the man we are hunting."

I wait a second to let the words sink in, then continue, "I was fortunate. The attacker was unable to accomplish his goal with me, though they did leave me a little memento of the encounter." I tap my neck where the tracker still resides, and say, "He left a tracker in my neck. It has already been used once to allow him to make a second attempt at taking my blood. Again, he was unsuccessful, this time thanks in part to my fellow team member and Tech Shift Marshal of the New Hopeland PD, Donal O'Brien. From the evidence gathered during this second attack, and some further investigation this gave rise to, we have been able to ascertain a number of key facts.

"First, this case is likely related to a historical case of a similar nature that took place in California two years ago. As such, the motive appears to be a greed-fuelled attempt at taking advantage of the current blood drive crisis. Second, the latest victim is a lady named Pauline Welch. Though she is sadly currently unable to answer queries... No, I am unable to disclose why she unavailable at this point in time. As I was saying, Miss Welch appears to have been fortunate enough to be only the second known victim to avoid having her blood sampled. Given not only the likelihood that this will lead to a repeat attempt, but that Miss Welch is currently staying at the New Hopeland Hospital, it has become imperative that we bring this matter to a close."

I fix my eyes dead ahead and wait a few seconds for the cameras present to zoom in like they usually do. In many ways, this is a standard technique for this sort of TV appearance. Right now, I have a second reason to do so. If he's watching, my hope is Doctor Sanderson is going to feel as if my eyes aren't fixed on a blank point on the back wall but are in fact locked with his.

"This is a message for the attacker. We *know* who you are now. We also know Miss Welch knows who you are. After tonight, we will be moving her to an undisclosed location, and her involvement will provide us with the proof we need to charge you for your crimes. Tonight, to ensure the safety of our key witness, the entire team will be waiting for you with Pauline Welch. This is your last opportunity. Come to us. Turn yourself in or try again. Either way, you're finished."

I depart the podium, and Hoove returns to his place. "Thank you all for coming. I am afraid we have no time for questions, as we have to make our final preparations for tonight. You may all leave."

OF COURSE, THE reporters protested. They wanted more than we gave them. That doesn't matter, though. Providing our target got the message that we're on to him, it's job done. If we're lucky—or maybe unlucky—we'll also get an answer to the question of whether there's more than one LV in the city. *It's a shame her boss didn't send Lori along, though,* I muse.

The room clears quickly enough for us to make good time getting ready to leave, at least. Lieutenant Hanson went ahead before the press event so that she could relieve Corporal Devereaux from his guard duty. That leaves me, Hoove, and Donal to ride in the back of the TS van. What surprises me is the sheer amount of ammo we've been cleared to carry. "Seems like overkill," I say.

"I still have my doubts that there are many people using the LV suits in New Hopeland, *if* there's more than one at all. But it's better to be prepared," Hoove replies. "Plus, if we're right, then Sanderson isn't going to be happy seeing this much firepower coming into the hospital. And if we're wrong, the chances are the real attacker will be watching anyway. The more nervous we can make him the better."

"Aye. A bit of fear goes a long way," Donal adds.

"That's part of the reason for the TS Unit, isn't it?" I ask. "Bringing on some fear?"

"Nothing like a werewolf attack to make ya shite yourself," Donal replies.

"You say that, but the TS Unit has a couple of full animal types, doesn't it? Wasn't it three hybrids, including yourself, and two animals? I know they're bigger than domestic animals, but I doubt most would make the association for the two."

Donal shrugs. "There are five of us, you're right there. We all have both types of TS gear, though."

"You do?"

"I thought that was public knowledge," Hoove says.

"Big difference between public knowledge and public known," I grunt, slightly annoyed at myself for not being aware of something that was apparently obvious.

"Bah. You haven't had a reason to know," Donal reassures me. "I'd reckon that most people have different figures in their head as to how it balances out. Fact is, we just use the TS gear that's most suited to any situation. The hybrid suits work best in most cases, but there have been times when going full animal is better. If we're potentially working in smaller areas, or if we need to blend in around real animals, for example. And I know that sounds stupid, but people tend to see what they expect to see, so if one or two dogs are bigger than the rest, they brush it off as genetics, if the lighting's right."

"Makes sense. The reasoning behind the dual types *and* how you get away with it. It must be a pain to learn to use both types, though."

"Not really," Donal says, relaxing against the wall on his side of the van. "The lower legs are the same in both types, so once you learn one, you can control the other just fine, even if the alignment of it changes between styles. The front legs on the animal ones are a little more difficult, but you can pick it up easy enough if you put the time in."

"My partner runs a local TS meet," I reply. "I've only been to a few, but it always amazes me how easily everyone moves in TS gear. They're all full animal there."

"I'd guess they're mostly second F's then, right?" I nod, knowing he means Fetishists, and he crosses his arms behind his head. "Honestly, if you want it enough, it doesn't take long to adjust with it. The beauty of the system is it's so straightforward. On top of that, TS gear is built to prevent you toppling over, did you know that?"

"Yeah, actually. Lori showed me the inside of the legs on her suit once. The back-leg locks with a heel pressure pad, and the front with the hand rest, eh?"

"That's right. Lori. That your partner?"

"Yeah."

"If you're dating a Tech Shifter, that explains why you weren't completely thrown when you first saw me suited up. Most people get a little creeped."

"Honestly? It surprised me that I wasn't. After the stuff when the gear first went out to the public, I've always been a little nervous around Tech Shifters. I guess I'm just getting used to it. Okay, here's a question then. What's the difference between an enforcement grade suit and a public one? I mean, I know a few differences, but I'm sure there's more to it."

"Hmm...am I allowed to talk about that?" Donal asks, turning to Hoove.

Hoove shrugs and gives his moustache a scratch. "Don't see why not. It's not public release detail, but Caz ain't gonna spread it about, are ya?"

"Of course not. I'm curious, is all."

"Well, weight is one thing," Donal replies. "Enforcement suits are heavier because they have a couple of layers of ballistic armour built in. The rest is how the parts work. You must have noticed the teeth, right?"

I nod. "The claws too. It all looks bigger and sharper than the ones at the meets."

"Aye. They're built for combat and rescue."

"Rescue?" I repeat, making the word a question.

"Public TS gear looks good, but unless you're modding it or already real strong, you wouldn't be able to do much damage with it. More than without it, sure, but not much. The reason for that is because the hydraulics are all in the locking mechanisms for the legs. For enforcement grade stuff, we have smaller systems built into the hands and muzzles too. You probably didn't notice, but the hands on my hybrid suit are actually a little lower down than my actual hands. It works with a motion mapping system, and if I give the right finger signals, the hands will get some extra oomph to them. Means I can rip stuff away if someone's trapped, or make sure a perp doesn't get away if I think they'll be hard to handle otherwise. Same goes with the jaw. A bit of extra pressure works wonders."

"Jaws of life," I say with a wink.

Donal laughs. "And death if it comes to it. If it hadn't been for the infrasound, or whatever the guy did, he wouldn't have gotten away when I grabbed him without unmasking first. Here's one to see how much attention you've been paying then. How can you immediately tell if someone's wearing an enforcement suit rather than a public one?"

"Not a clue."

"It's the tail," Hoove cuts in, obviously bored with not being part of the conversation. "Unless the wearer has a custom build that demands it, public suits come with tails as default, enforcement ones don't. The hydraulics aid with balance, so the tail isn't needed for anything other than aesthetics. That's how you can tell most of the time."

"Ya know," I say, thinking back to the first time I saw Donal suited up. "I don't think I even noticed that you didn't have a tail."

"Most don't. Like I said, people see what they expect to see."

"So, which F are you? I don't mind if you don't want to answer."

"None of them," Donal says with a smile.

"He's an A," Hoove adds.

"An A?"

"Yup. Donal ain't a Furry, Fetishist, or Freak, at least to my knowledge. Not that it would matter if he was any but the latter. He's just ambitious."

"The Captain here told me I couldn't expect too much in the way of promotion opportunities with the cases I had under my belt, but given my build and general attitude, he'd be happy to put me forward to lead the new TS Unit if I was willing to put the time in."

"Seriously? You went TS just to get a promotion?"

"You haven't seen his pay packet," Hoove snorts. "He earns the extra money too."

"I don't doubt it," I say, still unable to keep the surprise off my face.

"I tell ya what," Donal says, eying something at my waist. "Did Captain Hoover here explain how that thing works?"

I follow Donal's line of sight to my police issue HK45. "He did. Why's that?"

"How's your balance?" Donal asks Hoove.

Hoove sighs and gets up, taking a moment to get in synch with the rocking of the van. "Fine." He looks at me and adds, "Take the clip out before you do this. Last thing I want is my cause of death to read 'road bump related gun accident.'"

I do as I'm told and rise to my feet when Donal beckons me to. "Now," he says, "Take a solid stance...good. Put your glove on, point the gun at Captain Hoover, and let it get a lock on him."

Again, I do as I'm told.

"Now, watch this," Donal says, getting to his feet and turning to face the captain. He steps right in front of me, blocking Hoove from view completely. "You still got the gun up?"

"Yeah," I reply.

"Try firing. Like, really try. It's better not to teach yourself to hold back."

I try to pull the trigger, but it locks in place. I can feel a slight pull on the glove, but it doesn't go far. "It won't fire. Is that because of the clip being disengaged, or your being in the way?"

"Me," Donal replies. "Once it locks onto someone, it won't allow you to fire at anyone else until the targeting clears, either through a lack of action for two minutes or your removing your hand from the gun. It still has him tracked for now, though. Since the gun's not loaded, I'll show ya another trick. Try again the second I step out of the way."

I watch and wait, and after a few seconds, Donal darts to the side. I pull the trigger before I register that Hoove has moved, but the gun is way ahead of me, and my hand lurches towards the back corner of the van, where Hoove has sandwiched himself. This time, the trigger pulls too, making me glad the gun isn't loaded. I pull the gun up and study it, a new appreciation for the tool growing. "Neat."

"Pretty good, isn't it?" Donal says. "As long as you get a lock on, you can use a bit of misdirection like that. It's a basic trick, but it works well, especially when you have something big in front of you."

"I'll remember that."

We all feel the van come to a stop, and the green light goes on above the hatch. "We're here," the driver says, and the light goes off again.

"All right. Let's see how things are coming along," Hoove says, and starts marching towards the van door.

DOCTOR SANDERSON IS not a happy man. I'm far enough away from the room he's grabbed to rant at Hoove in that I can't hear him, but his body language is enough to give away how he feels. That Hoove isn't even giving him the courtesy of a polite nod doesn't appear to be helping either. I can't help but smile at that.

"Ol' Harold is on form," comes a voice from behind me.

I turn my head to see I'm not the only one taking some pleasure in Doctor Sanderson's torment. The desk I'm leaning on was unoccupied when I got here but is now manned by a single woman. She's decked out in the standard nursing scrubs most of the staff here seem to wear. I've never quite been certain whether they're blue, green, or something in between. I'm sure it's part of the dress code, but I do question her decision to tie her black hair back in a tight ponytail. The single braid that it's been pulled into would look nice were it not for the effect the whole style has achieved. Quite aside from the purple tints at the tips appearing a little odd in their current position, she has a wild look in her eyes. And I mean *really* wild. Were her hair hanging down, it would probably serve as a distraction. The sad thing is, I can't tell whether her smile is hungry or just pleasant but unfortunately set off by her eyes. I do get the impression she'd probably be quite pretty were she relaxed, though. I guess that's hospital work for you.

"Looks like it," I reply, turning my attention back to the silent movie argument.

"Still, can't blame him, can you? I can't remember the last time a hospital *didn't* have a bed crisis, so all this moving people about must be pretty rough for him. Especially given the condition of some of the patients."

*Was that a dig at us wonderful enforcers of the law? Let's test that a little.* I turn and offer a handshake. "Cassandra Tam, PI."

The woman wraps her hand around mine with a weird flourish, gripping with one finger at a time. "Denise Bridges, and I know."

"Denise, huh? Your name tag says A Bridges."

"Ooh, you *are* observant," she giggles. "I like trying out different names to see who's paying attention. It's a fun little game. I had one of the janitors calling me Karen all last week. As to my real name, it's Anabelle."

"Anabelle Bridges. Noted. And as far as moving the patients goes, I can't say I'm too happy about it either. Unfortunately, we don't have much choice in the matter. It was this or leave them in the line of fire and, as you already pointed out, some of them aren't in great condition. A little upheaval is better than letting them get caught up in this."

"Sounds like this guy you're after is pretty dangerous."

"He is."

"Still, how likely is it that the patients would be caught in the middle of it all? I mean, I'd have thought you're pretty good with a gun, being in your line of work. And the police? They must be practising a lot, right? If it's like you said on the TV, this guy's only after two people specifically."

I turn back and raise an eyebrow Anabelle's way. "Your point is?"

"My point is, we're not just dealing with physical trauma here. Some of the patients on this ward are suffering from the mental effects of their conditions too. Moving them isn't going to help that any."

"Nor is letting them get caught up in a gunfight with this guy. Frankly, if they're suffering emotionally, that makes their presence even more problematic."

"Is that right? Has it got something to do with those tinted contact lenses you're all wearing? Well, all but the big guy. I do love a brogue."

"I'll be sure to point you out to him," I reply, rolling my eyes. "And no, these are a charity thing. They don't affect the vision, so we can keep them in while on the job."

"Charity, huh? Which one? Doughnuts for Retired Po-Po?"

I let my eyes relax into my natural glare and ask, "Anabelle, are you trying to piss me off? I get that this is an awkward amount of upheaval for you all, but I can assure you it is absolutely necessary. If there were another option, we would have gone with it."

"Now, *that* I believe," she says, giving me a surprisingly disarming smile. "In response, yes I *am* trying. But only because I knew you were lying. I have ears, and Harold has a voice. I know the mugger is using some sort of light show to...confuse victims, I guess. And if you get that this is an awkward amount of upheaval as you put it, then you also need to understand this. We know you're just doing your jobs, but so are we. We're understaffed, overworked, and now being forced into consolidating our overcrowding problem into one harder to manage floor."

I look Anabelle up and down. Her breathing has quickened slightly, but she's not as angry as her tone would have me believe. Okay, let's try something less aggressive. "Feel better?" I try, carefully keeping my voice neutral.

"Absolutely. Don't you? It's better to address the elephant than to leave it in the room, don't you think?"

I shrug. "Sure, why not. For what it's worth, we're only here for the one night. And I'm sure Captain Hoover could be persuaded to supply some people to help with putting things back the way they were after we're done."

"Let's see how this all plays out first. If things get too out of hand, I doubt anyone, patients *or* staff, are gonna want to see you lot around for a while."

"Fair enough."

"Well," she replies, grabbing some papers from behind the desk. "Back to work. You should go get ready too. It's gonna be a long night."

I nod and give a polite wave but keep my eyes on Anabelle as she sets off down the adjacent hall.

"That looked fun," Donal says, stepping up beside me. "Get her number?"

"Happily taken, remember? Besides," I reply, giving him a playful slap on the shoulder, "she prefers big Irishmen."

And on that note, I head off to find Hanson and Devereaux and check out Pauline Welch's current condition.


THEY MAY NOT be happy with the arrangement, but to their credit, the hospital staff do a fine job of moving the majority of the patients to the presumed safety of the floor below before the night truly sets in. There are still a couple of critically ill patients up here with us, due to the simple fact that moving them would genuinely carry a high risk. As luck would have it, they're all already in private rooms with lockable doors. The plan is for three doctors to run hourly checks, relay style. Unless we've signalled them not to come knocking, they'll take it in turns to come up and check each patient one by one, accompanied of course by a member of the team each time.

The one exception to this rule is Pauline Welch who we're hoping will act as a suitable bait to lure out Doctor Sanderson, or indeed whoever else it may be if we're wrong. In keeping with this, her room is fully open. Each of us will be sitting guard with her for an hour at a time. The current working theory is that LV48, as we're now calling him, likely won't try anything while either Donal or I are there as he's already had a mixed bag of luck with us. This being the case, I take the first shift, sitting alone with nothing but the steady *beep* of Pauline's heart monitor for company until Doctor Sanderson drops by with his escort, Captain Hoover.

"You drew first shift too, eh?"

"Quite," Sanderson replies, as he checks over Pauline's unconscious body. I watch closely to make sure he doesn't do anything he shouldn't and am almost disappointed when he doesn't.

*You must be* really *bored if you're wishing harm on a victim. Get over it,* I admonish myself.

Sanderson and Hoove soon move on, and I'm alone with my thoughts again. Assuming we're right, no attack is going to come until after Sanderson finishes his walk around the halls. Plus however long it takes him to get ready.

Pushing myself back into the annoyingly uncomfortable chair the hospital has supplied for us does nothing to lighten my mood, so I start playing with my earphones instead. They're slightly oversized, over-the-ear ones like you'd get at a shooting gallery. We decided we needed to be able to hear each other, at least when any attack first starts, so we're all wearing them around our necks at the moment. There were a few pairs that would double up as radios at the station too but, aside from there not being enough of them for all of us, there was always the risk that the microphone would pick up the infrasound, so complete silence and a starting position of sound-blocking-necklace it is. It means I can press my finger against one side, push it back, and let it spring back into place again, creating an almost satisfying *thud* as it clashes with its opposite side. The real fun comes in trying to get the sound to synch up with the heart monitor, either at the same time as a *beep* or directly between two.

"Yeah, 'cause that's a great party game," I grumble to myself.

*There are shadows in the hospital.* I slap myself on the cheeks with both hands. *Of course there are, idiot. There are shadows everywhere. You just need the right lighting.*

"This floor is huge," I tell myself, leaning forward to rest my elbows on my knees and my face in my hands. "I bet the floor patrols are a lot more fun than this."

I groan. *Because fighting a modern-day vampire is such fun, eh? This must be torture if you're begging to star in your own horror movie.*

"Damn right it is."

I try to relax a little, letting my mind focus on the rhythmic sound of the heart monitor again.

*Beep...beep...beep.*

I'm letting a combination of boredom and fear get the better of me, which is not good for any of us. It also means something I hadn't noticed is eating at me.

*Beep...beep...beep.*

I just need to relax. Relax, and figure out what specifically has got me so wired.

*Beep...beep...beep.*

I look over at Pauline Welch, lying still on the bed next to me, and shake my head. "You've got the easiest job of all of us."

"Good listener, isn't she?"

I look up and see Corporal Devereaux standing in the doorway. "Don't mind me, I'm bored, is all."

"I hear you. The shift earlier was only bearable 'cause there were so many people passing through. No such luck tonight, eh? Say, could you give me a hand?"

"Sure," I reply and push to my feet. "What's up?"

He leads me out through the door and, to my surprise, he has a small table waiting. "If you could grab the coffee and the box, that'd be great. I almost dropped them carrying the table over here."

I do as he asks, and he grabs the table by the edge and pulls it into the room. With Devereaux not bothering to lift it this time, it makes a ridiculously noisy scraping sound all the way up until he gets it in position to the side of the chair. He takes the drink and the small box from me and says, "Thanks, Cassie."

"So, what's in the box?" I ask, leaning myself into the doorframe to steady myself while I try to loosen up my legs a little.

"Cards," he replies, dumping them onto the table. "Figured I may as well play some solitaire while we wait for the fireworks to start. Speaking of which, you can consider yourself relieved."

I stifle a yawn and say, "Thanks. I'll get whoever does the next escort session to bring you another drink if you like."

"Sounds good. Coffee would be great. White, with sugar."

"Got ya." I give my arm another stretch, add, "Catch you later," and leave to check in with the others.


"EVENING, CASSIE, FANCY meeting you here," Lieutenant Hanson says from behind the desk when she sees me walk around the corner. "Hope you're not in for anything serious."

"Dehydration," I reply, making a beeline for the hot drinks machine at the back of the waiting room.

"Probably shouldn't go for coffee then. That'll dry you right out."

"Too bad I'm prone to bad decisions then."

"Well, I won't argue with you on that one. How's Welch doing?"

I take a mouthful of something black and caffeinated that's masquerading as coffee and stroll over to the desk.

"I'm a detective, not a doctor. The *beep-beep* is nice and steady, though, so that's probably a good thing, right?"

"Probably," Hanson agrees. "You all set for your patrol?"

"Trying to get rid of me already? I hope you're not planning to sneak the good Corporal away from his post."

"Nah, Dev's far too serious for that. Besides, Hoove'll be due back soon. I wouldn't want to give him a heart attack, or they might *force me* into his job."

I snort out a laugh and ask, "Any sign of anything yet? Or anything in particular I should check?"

"Donal didn't mention anything on his first walk-through. But with Sanderson doing the first rounds, we expected that. Sounds like it takes a while to get through it all."

"Yeah. First walk-through is a good chance to get a look at potential entry points, so it'll take longer than any subsequent ones. Unless the other forty-seven LVs turn up en masse, of course."

"Don't tempt fate," a voice says from the door leading back to what we've been calling the central hub, and Captain Hoover walks over to join us at the desk. He looks down at my cup and wrinkles his nose at the sight of the black goop I'm now struggling to convince myself to take another mouthful of. He reaches behind his back and pulls out a small Thermos, which he waves at me. "I'll stick with my soup."

"You are such an old man," Hanson laughs.

Hoove flicks her ear and replies, "One of us has to act our age. Now, go rest up in the staff room."

Hanson gets to her feet and gives a playful salute, then heads off to the room Hoove and Sanderson were arguing in earlier. "I better start my patrol," I say, lifting my cup. "Maybe it'll make me tired enough to finish this thing."

"Keep your eyes open," Hoove replies and settles back into the chair, his eyes going to the computer monitor in front of him.

This floor of the hospital encompasses several different departments. It's set out so that there's a central hub with various elevators and hallways leading to other sections, all technically on the same *level* as this one, but classed officially as different floors. We had considered bringing in other members of the PD to help us patrol the entire thing, but it would have taken a long time to get anyone new up to speed. On top of that, if we can enclose the potential encounters in one smaller area, it's a lot easier to manage.

The layout is easy enough to get to grips with. A single door at the end of a short hallway leads to the hub area. At our end of this is the main desk where I had the run-in with Nurse Bridges. From here, there's a large open-plan area that acts as a waiting room, with a couple of smaller rooms lining the back wall. These amount to storerooms, minor consultation rooms, and the aforementioned staff room. A hallway reaches out from either side of the room, and wraps around in a large square, leading off to multiple different areas. Pauline Welch is in an individual room in the North Western corner, and the other remaining critical patients are spread out. These rooms are almost all on the outer side of the corridor, while the inner wall consists mostly of a mix of small rooms set aside for specialist procedures and one large, open-plan room, which is where we moved most of the patients from.

My first stop on the trip is the hallway to the right of the waiting room. The first door I come to here leads to the open-plan area. I nudge the door ajar and peer in, but don't enter. There's another door on the opposite side, and our agreed route is to check in one side, but not enter until we reach the other. Happy there's no clear danger, I let the door swing shut and keep walking. Most of the patients on this side had private rooms but were suitable for moving. As a result, we've locked pretty much every door in the hallway other than the one I just looked into. The locks can only be opened from the outside, we checked that. The reasoning was that if a patient could unlock it from the inside, they could also lock it, which isn't something the staff want to deal with. I give the doors a quick examination anyway to make sure they're still locked, but that doesn't take too long. I glance in on our one guest on the hall as I pass their window. It's an elderly man wearing breathing apparatus who looks about as comfortable as you'd expect given the circumstances. "Think I'll save those checks for escort duty," I mumble as I reach the left turn to take me towards the northeast section.

The inner wall is devoid of doors for the first third of its length, which means all I have to do is check on that side for signs of alternative entry points. There's nothing obvious. The outer wall is mostly given over to private rooms and a couple of consultation rooms, all of which are also locked. Being thorough, I not only test the doors but look in through any windows I come by. Right now, I'm finding nothing but desks, and empty spaces where beds were until we disrupted everything.

Once I clear the area enclosing the open-plan area, doors start to appear on the inner wall again. The first is locked, but the second is open. I expected that. This, we were told, leads to the floor's operating theatres, and doesn't have a lock. Inside is a longer hallway spanning the entire length of the inner section. There are four operating theatres in total, and our instructions are to check two on this side, then the other two when we reach the other side of the square hallway. Both the ones I go into are near identical and may as well have been ripped from TV shows. The medical implements are locked up in drawers, which doesn't help if we're right about Doctor Sanderson, and everything is ridiculously but necessarily sterile. The main thing is there are no additional entry points. I spot a basket of what I'm guessing is dirty laundry close to what will be the last theatre I check on the other side, and decide to leave it there for that run.

Further up the main hallway, I find a locked janitor's closet, and a few more locked consultation rooms, then hit the left turn to the hallway that leads to the northwest side of the floor. By this time, it's all feeling a bit rinse and repeat. The only difference up here is a few windows face out towards the other parts of the building you can reach via the hub. Below us is a picturesque courtyard. Most of the windows are solid without any means of opening them, and the ones that do open are too small to fit a person through. The exceptions to these rules are the ones at each end of the hallway and directly in the middle.

The inner wall contains four alternative entrances to the operating theatre area. In this case, they lead to observation areas, one for each theatre. These are nothing more than small rooms with large platforms at the back that give you a clear view of the adjoining theatre via the large windows built into the walls. Pauline Welch's room is in the northwest corner, and I give a quick look-in as I pass. Corporal Devereaux seems happy enough with his card game, and I don't stick around too long, though I do use the small bin in the room for my now empty cup of gross. Locked doors are my friend all the way up until the door to the operating theatre hallway. I enter, just as I did last time, and am unsurprised to find both rooms are fine.

In the hallway, there's a metal opening in between the centre theatres. This, as I recall, leads down to the laundry room. The laundry basket to its right sits next to the door to the last theatre I came to when I checked from the other side... *Was that always there? If it was up by this door, I'd have seen the laundry chute. Guess I must have misjudged it... I blame the lighting.*

I walk over to the basket and open it up. There are a couple of sets of scrubs at the bottom, but nothing else. On my way back up the hallway, I stop to skim-read the message board fixed to the wall opposite the laundry chute. It's an old-style thing containing handwritten notes about rota shifts. In a way, I'm glad it's not a modern touch screen installation. If the staff are as overworked as they claim, they may as well spend the budget on useful things like medical equipment rather than hi-tech message walls. As it is, there's nothing worth noting on the various pieces of paper.

I enter the outer hallway once again and continue my rounds. Locked doors remain my constant companion until I finally reach the door to the open-plan area. This time, when I nudge the door open, I walk in.

I can tell straight away that I may as well have not bothered. I've not had to stay in the New Hopeland Hospital before, nor have I had to visit anyone in a ward like this. The whole thing is laid out as I expected, with spaces set aside for beds. But rather than the metal framework and pull-apart blinds you see on vintage TV shows, this is a mix of spaces with no divides, and those with hard-looking cubicle structures identical to the ones you find in a lot of offices. Sure, you can pull something across the front for complete privacy, but rather than a curtain, it's a reinforced series of plastic plates. In total, I count thirty bed areas along the wall that adjoins the waiting area, and twenty-eight on the wall closest to the operating theatre hallway. Here, the beds are divided in the middle by another manual note board.

The side walls have a few more cubicles, and the middle of the room is taken up by yet more bed zones, and a couple of desks I'm assuming are set aside for staff. There are no obvious points of entry other than the two doors at either end. It's all very dull, dark and empty. *At least it looks different to the rooms I've seen already.*

I walk back out the door I came in through and head back to the desk where Hoove is sitting. "Catch anything on the security cameras?" I ask.

Hoove shakes his head and looks up from the screen. "Just you walking around and Donal starting his rounds with Nurse Bridges. I hear you two are well acquainted already."

I smile. "We spoke earlier."

"The way she tells it, it was a bit more than that."

"She gave me some attitude, and I gave some back. Nothing too serious."

Hoove laughs, and relaxes back into the chair, crossing his arms behind his head. "To be honest, I'm more worried about Donal with her. She was *real* happy to have *him* escorting her."

"I thought she might be," I reply, moving around to watch the monitors for a minute.

"Even suited up like he is, it's the accent apparently. It gets worse. The cheesy bastard told her the name Anabelle suits her. See if you can guess why."

I shrug. "Not a clue."

"Because she's a doll and he wants to possess her."

I turn to look at Hoove and, after a few seconds studying him, realise he's serious. I crack first, but soon enough, we're both laughing our asses off.

Finally, Hoove brings us back to reality by asking, "So, did *you* find anything?"

"No," I reply, forcing the laughter back down again. "There are a couple of potential entry points, the windows at the back and maybe the laundry chute between the operating theatres, but we knew about them already. Everything else seems fine. The doors that should be locked are, and the ones that shouldn't be aren't. For now at least, we're fine."

"Well, let's see how long that lasts."

I glance down at the monitor and see a shot of just outside the room we have Pauline Welch in. Though we don't have a clear view of the inside of the room, the angle does allow us to see the edge of the table Corporal Devereaux is presumably still playing cards on. I spot his feet underneath that, crossing and uncrossing as he stretches.

And something is still gnawing at me.

I narrow my eyes. "He was quick..."

"Who was?"

"Doctor Sanderson. When he checked in on Pauline Welch, he was quick."

Hoove pours some soup from his Thermos into the lid, gives it a quick blow, then takes a mouthful. "Of course he was. He's not likely to try anything while we're escorting him."

"No, but that's the thing. He..."

Hoove raises a hand to silence me, and I follow his gaze to Donal O'Brien and Nurse Bridges as they return from their tour of our guests. "Everything okay?" Hoove asks.

"Seems to be," Donal replies. He looks down to Nurse Bridges and asks, "Anything you noticed?"

"Nope. Most of them are resting soundly. One or two are awake and worried, but that's to be expected."

"Okay, good," Hoove says.

"Well, I better get back downstairs," Anabelle says with a yawn. "Long night ahead and all that."

Hoove waves her on, and we all watch silently as she makes her way down the hallway to the hub. Once she's gone, Donal turns to us and asks, "So, what's going on then? Ya shut up pretty quickly when you saw us coming."

"I was just saying that Doctor Sanderson didn't try anything while he did his rounds."

"And like *I* said," Hoove replies, "he wouldn't. Not while we were with him."

"Exactly. And when have we *not* been with him?"

Both Hoove and Donal go quiet, and when Donal does respond, his voice is low and slow. "Pretty much all the rest of the time."

"That's what I've been missing. What we've all been missing. If he wants Pauline Welch's blood, he'll have already taken it. Tonight, that won't be his aim."

"We've put a fucking death sentence on her head," Hoove growls. "Okay, let's mix things up a bit. We'll have two people on the desk at all times and stagger the patrols with the escort runs rather than mix them. And we'll have two people in with Welch at all times."

"So who goes now?" I ask.

"I'll do it," the Captain replies, getting to his feet and downing his soup like most people down beers. "In the meantime, one of you wake Hanson and send her on her patrol. When the next one turns up..." He picks up a piece of paper and reads down the names, then continues, "Doctor Thorndike it says here. When they turn up, hold off on the tour until Hanson's back. We'll wait for Caz to finish her tour, then switch me and Devereaux for Hanson and O'Brien."

"Got it," Donal replies, and Hoove starts off on a jog towards the left-hand hall at the back of the room. Donal stretches his arm and flexes the claws on his Tech Shift gear, then says, "I'll go wake Sleeping Beauty."

I'm about to suggest I should do it, but Donal's obviously been waiting for a moment like this, because he clears the room at speed. With little else I can do, I just sit back and wait for the shocked scream from the room we were supposed to be using as a rest area.

MY PATROL COMES a little under an hour later. Unlike his two counterparts for the evening, Doctor Thorndike is a kindly old man who is probably a few years past retirement age. Despite his advanced age, he moves quickly and efficiently through the halls and carries out his checks with the minimum of fuss. As a result, we reach Pauline Welch's room very quickly.

"Captain Hoover?" he asks, offering a hand to New Hopeland's ultimate moustache wielder. The Captain nods and accepts the greeting. Thorndike turns to Corporal Devereaux then and adds, "And you are Corporal Devereaux, I understand?"

"Sure am," Devereaux replies.

Thorndike nods and starts checking over the heart monitor. "It is good to see that the police do not have our problems with attracting younger staff. I do believe our youngest staff member is in their late forties."

"No way is Nurse Bridges in her forties," I comment.

"Nurse Bridges?" Thorndike stops mid-thought and frowns. "This is unusual."

"What's wrong?" I ask.

"This isn't one of the regular heart monitors. It's an older model than we normally use now. Unless…I suppose we could have set this up in case anything happened. It's certainly more disposable. Though I really should have been told… Unreliable little things, though. Would anyone object if I checked the finger connector?"

"Go right ahead," Hoove says, his face taking on a suddenly very serious expression.

Thorndike reaches down and takes Welch's hand. He pauses, frowns again, and removes the finger connector.

*Beep…beep…beep.*

We all watch the monitor screen, waiting for it to stop displaying a heartbeat.

*Beep…beep…beep.*

"Her hand is cold," Thorndike comments. "And her breathing…"

"Looks fine to me," Devereaux says. "Steady rise and fall of the chest."

Thorndike shakes his head. "Most people breathe with their abdomen when they rest. Not all, mind you, but still."

"Check her," Hoove says.

Doctor Thorndike slowly peels the bedding down and one thing starts to become clear. When he rolls down the top of Pauline Welch's hospital gown, it's confirmed. Strapped to her torso is a small machine simulating the rise and fall of her chest. Doctor Thorndike brings his fingers to the woman's neck and, after a few seconds, shakes his head. "She's dead."

"How long?" Hoove asks.

"That is hard to say. Her body is at room temperature already, though." He raises the fingers he used to check the pulse, revealing a smear of foundation. "Cosmetics. She's not stiff, which means she's been dead more than thirty-six hours. If someone has been taking steps to hide discoloration...that shouldn't happen earlier than the second day. She arrived yesterday, or possibly the evening before as I recall."

"Unconscious too," I say. "Any chance she was dead already?"

"No, someone would have noticed. She had a procedure, though. Someone must have checked in on her during and after that..."

All at once, all the lights on the floor cut.

# Chapter Eight

"DOCTOR THORNDIKE," HOOVE says, his voice low. "I want you to head to the nearest locked room. Get inside and lock the door."

"The doors only lock from the outside," he replies.

"I'll go with him," Devereaux says. "I can slide the key back under the door after it locks. That should eliminate anyone taking it from us. Assuming *we're* the targets, that should stop anyone trying to go for the Doc."

"Do it," Hoove orders. "Go without your torch if you can. I want a test on how hard it's gonna be to get around without being spotted."

Doctor Thorndike and Corporal Devereaux make their way into the hallway, and a little over a minute later, Devereaux returns on his own, his shape barely visible. "Sorry," he says. "He wanted to go to the staff area rather than a patient room."

"How's it looking out there?" Hoove asks.

"Too dark. Working without the torches will be difficult."

"Good job the HK45s won't be affected." Hoove places a hand on my shoulder—which I will claim *did not* make me jump or squeak—and adds, "It's unlikely our vampire knows we know about Welch yet. That means he may still be heading this way. Given Welch's heart monitor is still functioning, it's likely just the lights that have been cut, so the cameras should still be on. I want you to get to the front desk and rendezvous with Hanson and O'Brien. Try to figure out where Sanderson or whoever else this may be is and see if you can corral him."

I nod, even though no one can see me, and say, "Okay. Keep your headphones off as long as possible, though. We can call out if we need to."

"Sucks not to have radio contact," Devereaux says.

"Too bloody true," Hoove agrees and gives me a pat on the back. "Get going. Let's try to finish this quickly."

I walk out in silence, and turn right, placing my hand on the wall to feel my way down in the dark. No sense in drawing attention to myself unintentionally. As I make my way down the hallway, I listen intently to my surroundings. Nothing. Yet. My hand finds the corner, and I become grateful I left my arm outstretched a little, or my face would have found it too. Moving quicker, I clear the last section of the hallway and spot the light of the monitor behind the desk, the screen illuminating Hanson and O'Brien's face a little as they watch.

I walk over quickly, thankful we'd had the foresight to move the chairs against the walls. I make my way behind the desk and join the huddle. "Anything?"

"Other than you walking down the hallway?" Hanson asks. "*Nada*. How's our unconscious bait?"

"Dead. For a couple of days apparently," I reply, keeping my voice low. Hanson and Donal glance at each other and I continue, "Which means it'll likely be me who Sanderson heads for. So, if you don't mind, I'd like to find him sooner rather than later."

Hanson nods and taps a key on a holo-keyboard, and the view changes to a shot facing another corridor. The night vision isn't great, but it's enough to see if anything moves. Hanson lingers for a few seconds, then clicks to another shot, this time of the windows at the far end of the building. Next comes the windows further along, then another hallway, and another. When she clicks again, we get a shot of the main desk, the three of us sitting behind it. Something catches my eye out in the room, but it's gone before I can see what it is.

*Was that a light?*

"Hanson, can you click back to the shot of us again. I thought I saw something in the room, but I couldn't catch it."

"Hold on," Donal says and twitches a finger. He looks around, then says, "Nothing on my infrared."

"There was definitely something," I state.

Hanson shrugs. "Well, let's have a look." She clicks back to the shot of our room. Nothing on the camera other than us.

I sigh. "I'm gonna do something. Tell me what you see on screen."

I get up and walk forward, my eyes focused on a small green light. When I get as close to it as I can, I lift one finger towards it.

Hanson snorts out a laugh. "Nice."

"Move the camera on," I say, and within seconds, the light is gone.

"The cameras aren't on non-stop, only when they're on screen," I say, walking back to the desk.

"Makes no difference to us," Donal replies. "We'd only be able to see what's on screen anyway."

"Actually, this is bad," Hanson says. "At least if we're right about Sanderson."

Donal crosses his arms, his armoured face still angled at the screen. "How do ya mean?"

"If the green light comes on and goes off depending when the cameras are active," I clarify, "then that gives a signal for when we're watching. If Sanderson is our vamp, he'd know that and could be moving and hiding between shots. Where would he be able to cut the power from?"

Hanson clicks her tongue, thinking through her patrol. "Nowhere I spotted. Another floor, maybe?"

A muffled sound rings out through the dark, drawing our gaze to the wall at the back of the waiting room. As soon it registers where the sound likely came from, Hanson clicks through the cameras until she comes to the two set up in the open-plan area. They don't cover anything close to the whole room, but her clicking back forth every few seconds gives us a good shot at either catching movement or at least making any intruder too nervous to move.

"Go back," Donal says when Hanson switches camera again. "Now wait...what's that?"

We lean in to look at the part of the screen that he's tapping. "The back wall?" I try.

"Aye, but look closely. Isn't that the message board?"

"Looks like it... No, you're right, that's wrong. It shouldn't be that far to the side."

"Think we should check it out?" Hanson asks.

My lips twitch in and out of a grimace, understanding my thoughts before I do. "I'll do it. If he's in there, I may be able to entice him out. Keep an eye on the cameras in case he gets behind me."

I MAKE MY way to the entrance nearest to the western corridor. My thinking is if Welch *is* still the first target, I'll be close enough to them to run in and offer assistance. Just to make sure, I pause in front of my intended door. Silence. *Quit stalling, Cassie. Let's get this done.*

I sigh, and draw my HK45, flexing my fingers around the grip as I get a good feel for the weapon. I let my free hand drop to my waist and take the torch out of its holster on my belt. And that's when it hits me. "I can't grip the torch and still use the auto correction pad. *Diu.* Would it have been that hard to magnetise the torches to the guns? Okay...workarounds."

I feel the weight of the torch in my hand and think back to my days at the Police Academy in Vancouver. The neck-index technique, where you hold the torch ice pick-style by your face is the common one, but that doesn't resolve my grip issue for the HK. I could modify it by resting the torch between my head and neck, but that's gonna limit my neck movement, and start feeling really uncomfortable really quickly. The Rogers technique, where you hold the torch between the index and middle fingers, is out because the torch is too bulky, which sucks because it would have had me close to a two-handed grip on the gun.

Well, when all else fails, revert to the popular choice. I grip the torch ice pick-style in my left hand and bring it up underneath my right. It's almost cliché now given the number of TV shows depicting the style, but the Harries technique is popular for a reason. It's gonna be a more awkward transition when it comes to taking a two-handed approach to shooting, but I'll take it.

As of now, my plan is simple; use the torch until I can't. Then we'll see how good my night vision is. And so, I give the door a push and walk slowly inside, rotating at my core to pass the light over as wide an area as possible. I back myself into the door as it shuts and take a look to my left, watching the corners of the room on my side, but there's nothing in sight. With each step forward, I do a partial sweep, illuminating the insides of the bed areas as best I can.

*Careful*, I warn myself, my finger twitching on the trigger when the light catches the edge of a screen and casts a shadow across the wall. I keep moving, taking in my surroundings. Right now, there's only one sound I can hear: my own footsteps, which are about as quiet as I can make them. The problem is that in the near silence, they stand out more than they would in a nighttime street, which is a bit distracting. On the plus side, it means I'll likely hear if anyone else moves in here too.

I make my way around the side of the room closest to the entrance doors, slowly moving towards the Eastern entrance. A few more shadows spook me more than they need to, but I find nothing, so I move up to the Northern side of the room. This is where I'm expecting the action to come anyway. That's not to say investigating the southern side was a waste, nor was it me stalling. I need to familiarise myself with the area again, see what I can use if I need to, or what someone else could. It's not enough to give me an advantage, given we suspect a member of the hospital staff to be the LV, but it's enough to reduce the hindrance, at least.

I move along the room again and finally reach the main point of interest for us. Moving the torch up and down in front of me, I can see the message board has been shoved aside a little, and behind it is...a gap. I press myself against the wall and angle the torch towards the shadows, but I can't see inside. So, I wait and listen. Still silence. Which leaves me one option: go in blind.

My eyes drift down to my tie, not that I can see it right now. Like most of my collection, it appears to be plain black, unless you get close to it in good light. Today's design is a Bixie, a two-horned, winged lion that's supposed to keep evil at bay. I smile wryly to myself. I may not put much stock in superstitions, but I sure dress like I rely on them a lot.

*Well, that's all the protection you're getting.*

I slide my foot between the board and the gap and nudge it further aside. Either it's designed to move, it was only resting against the wall, or it's been removed, because it moves with ease. Once the gap is big enough, I step in and flash the torch from left to right. To my surprise, there's a whole room back here. There isn't much to it, and it's not very wide, but it's clearly important. The walls are lined with columns of switches, each labelled with simple codes; 1A, 1B, 1C and so on. At the back of the room is a single computer terminal, the screen lit brightly. I approach it with caution—because I learned my lesson with Pauline Welch's machine—and stare down at the screen. It's unlocked, that's clear, but my attempts to click on things bring up password prompts.

"Not touching that again," I grumble and scan what I *can* see. The screen shows a list of references, matching those on the walls, and they all have a green bar next to them. All except one: 4C. This reference has a red, flashing bar next to it. "We're on the fourth floor...this must be the power terminal. Where's the button...?"

I move along the walls until I come to 4C. Of course, one single switch in the column is facing a different way to the rest. I flick it back on, and the lack of response is hardly surprising. Best I can guess, the switch relates to the lights on the floor, and the red bar on the screen means it's now locked out from changing state. Assuming it was the vamp who did this, that would confirm he thinks we don't know about Welch. Cutting the power completely would leave her without the life-confirming heart monitor, so this helps the illusion.

I glance around the room again and notice the open door pushed back against the wall for the first time. If closed, it would be where the message board was. When I look at the wall opposite, there's another door pushed open, but the rear of the message board shows it's still in place. *Now...were the doors always hidden, or did the LV do that? We didn't take any of the pre-operation patrols into the operating theatre hall or the open-plan room, and none of the escort runs go there either, so...*

*Thud.*

My head turns instinctively towards the gap, and I raise my HK45 back into position. I take a deep breath and step quickly through the gap, and immediately turn towards where I thought the sound came from. The torchlight catches the visor on the LV's mask and I suddenly realise my mistake. My knees start to shake, and I collapse to the floor, instinctively tightening my grip on the gun, even as the torch clatters to the floor.

The room is spinning, guided by something barely audible to me. But I can still see the shape of my attacker as he walks towards me. Barely.

Acting quickly, I pull the headphones up over my ears, drowning the room in silence. The nausea begins to fade away, but with that comes the knowledge that the LV is almost upon me.

*You can use this. Drop forward and loosen your grip on the gun...there. Wait...just a little longer.*

The LV stops in front of me and slips two of his elongated fingers under the top of the headphones.

*Now!*

The instant I feel the headphones start to move away from my head, I force my entire body upwards and throw my hands out. I twist my knuckles towards the LV's head and grip the ear-like protrusions on his mask as low down as I can. With a guttural scream, I drop my core and pull with all my strength. The lump of metal in my right hand comes away with a crack, and the one in my left rips from the helmet, but remains attached, albeit hanging limply. Keeping moving, I drop the chunk from my right hand and twist my body back around, throwing a hard punch into the LV's gut.

The force of my strike pushes the LV back, but also causes me to overbalance and drop to one knee. I reach up, push the headphones off my ears, and wait. The nausea doesn't return, and nor do the barely registered sounds of before. Somewhere in the direction of Pauline Welch's room, I hear a gunshot. And then the LV in front of me laughs.

The laugh is a manic, whooping ball of crazy that I wasn't expecting. It's also very noticeably female.

Another gunshot.

I make a grab for my HK45, but the LV moves quicker and swings a heavily booted foot into my jaw. She ignores the gun and grabs me by the throat with the hand that doesn't include claws, dragging me to my feet. With the helmet looking too heavy for me to break without help, I go for what's already worked, and throw my body forward, lifting my knee into her mid-section. The grip on my throat loosens and I dive to the side, grabbing my torch from the floor.

*Click. Thud.*

I raise the light just in time to see the claws fall from the LV's hand. *No broken fang lights, both ears still present—before I took them out—and the number forty-nine on the forehead. Now I get it.*

"You're the one who attacked me the first time," I say, narrowing my eyes. I nod to the claws on the floor, and add, "Guess my blood isn't on the menu anymore, eh?"

The LV darts forward and catches me with a surprise left hook, snapping my head around and straight into the follow-up right. Another left follows, this time catching me in the gut and lifting me off the floor. I instinctively grip the torch tighter and, with a primal growl, I swing it butt-first into my attacker's helmet. The glass is obviously reinforced, as the impact does nothing more than create a dull *thwack*, and barely moves my foe. She fires back by grabbing my head and slamming her own into it.

I stumble back and barely get my arm over the top of one of the bed space dividers to stop myself falling.

*Definitely reinforced.*

A movement in the shadows catches my attention, and I grab the divider and pull it across me. I slam it into the LV's incoming fist but drop the torch again in the process. Thankfully, my eyes are adjusting, and I can at least make out her shape in the dark. *No, from the way she's gripping it, I missed her hand but caught her in the wrist. That's an opening.*

I shove the divider forward and she moves to avoid it, giving me the chance to slam my own fist into the side of her ribs. I feel her fold into it slightly, her arm moving down to block any follow-up attacks to the same spot. I expected that and angle my second punch at the opposite side. The LV hunkers down and catches me with another headbutt, but this one doesn't have as much behind it, and only knocks my head back rather than forcing me away.

Not wanting to lose the advantage, I lift my leg close to my chest and push out with a front kick that sends the LV tripping over the downed divider. She rolls to the side, narrowly avoiding my attempt at caving her ribs in with a hard boot, and grabs something from the floor. From the change in stance, I can tell what it is: the HK45. I freeze, playing along with the façade that she doesn't even know what she's walked into.

She laughs at me, and it's damn near a cackle. Even with the mask providing some muffling, I can hear how much she's enjoyed this. And she thinks she's going to enjoy her victory. This is why I didn't bring the Glock on this one. As much as I don't like the way the HK works, it *does* have some advantages. Like fingerprint recognition.

She squeezes the trigger.

The trigger locks.

I start to move again, but the gun smacks into my nose, causing me to bring my hand to my face. Even without the light, I can tell I'm bleeding.

The sound of a door opening and closing snaps me out of my introspection. I grab both the torch and the gun from the floor and dash across the room, heading in the direction of the sound and out into the corridor opposite Pauline Welch's. Up ahead, I see the doors leading to the hall outside the operating rooms swing shut, and give chase, torch and gun back into a comfortable Harries position. I take advantage of the way the doors swing both ways and kick them open, but slow on entry. The LV could be behind any of four doors, or even in the laundry chute.

I take two steps and stop.

*Knock. Knock. Knock.*

I do a full one-eighty and come face to face with something that will remain in my nightmares for years to come. The LV is attached to the wall above the swinging doors. She's just pressed up against it, her helmet angled directly at me. The whole image is so bizarre that it causes me to react far slower than I should.

*Hum.*

The LV launches forward from the wall, tackling me to the floor. I try to roll on top, but she uses the momentum to throw me off and into the wall shoulder first, then scrambles out from under me. She throws a kick at my face, but I dodge it and dive forward, tackling her in the stomach. The LV adapts quickly, however, and gets her arms under my own. One twist of her body later, and I feel the impact of the door behind me, followed by a short rush of air as I stumble back, struggling to remain upright.

I raise the HK and attempt to get a lock on, but the LV ducks and weaves as she moves, and shoves me over the nearby operating table. An idea hits me shortly after the floor does the same, and I change my grip on my gun, switching the barrel into my hand. As I get to my feet, I listen. The LV is either getting pissed off, or overconfident, because she isn't even trying to hide her footsteps right now. So, I swing a gun-assisted spinning back fist, slamming the butt of the gun into the side of her helmet.

"The gun is mightier than the torch," I mutter, following the LV as the impact forces her towards the operating table. I tackle her down and, dropping the torch onto her chest, wrap a hand around her throat. As I'd hoped, she brings both her own hands up to try to force my one away. Roaring like a lunatic, I start slamming the butt of the gun down on her helmet at speed with my stronger arm. She reacts quickly and tries to move her hands. I tighten my grip on her throat. When that causes her to panic and increase her struggling, I lean into my grip a little more, still slamming the gun against her helmet, over and over again.

*Crack.*

"Got you."

Her hand comes up and brushes my wrist, guiding it beyond the helmet and causing me to overbalance and go sprawling across her. She starts bringing her knee up, trying to catch my head, ribs, anything. They aren't hard strikes, but the one that catches my arm is enough to make me lose my grip on her throat.

And just like that, she's able to shove me away again and start towards the door. Unwilling to give her a chance to set up some other trick like she did with the wall, I force myself forward and slam into her back as she exits the room. She crashes face first into the opposite wall, creating another satisfying *crack*, but shifts her weight and throws herself backwards, crushing me against the other wall. A wildly thrown elbow stumbles me sideways, and a right hook drops me.

Even as I fall, I switch grips again and raise the HK45. The LV, unaware that I'm still conscious, tries to open the door to the power room, only to find it locked. She tilts her masked face, making two of us who are confused by it all. Before either of us can dwell on it, though, the HK45 light goes green, signalling that I have a lock. I squeeze the trigger.

The impact of the bullet as it hits the LV's leg sends her into a desperate whirl as she presses herself back against the wall to keep herself upright. She reaches her hand down and presses her fingers to the wound, then brings them back up to her face. Her head turns towards me and time seems to freeze.

One by one, the lights in the hallway turn on, and like an idiot, I look up at them. Realising what I've done, I try to find the LV again, but am barely in time to see her head disappear down the laundry chute.

"*Diu*," I grunt, and push myself up to my feet and dash for the chute. For a moment, I consider following her down.

*Crash.*

I raise my gun again and point it directly at the new LV that's been shoved through the door at the end of the hall. This one has a missing ear, marking it as the one Bert attacked. Before I can get a lock on him, he twists his body and throws Lieutenant Hanson at me.

"Fucking bastard," Lieutenant Hanson growls, scrambles to her feet, and hurtles back down the hall.

Everything is happening too fast for me to try to get a safe lock on. *Okay, let's haul ass.*

I sprint away from the LV, exiting via the door I came in through and making a quick turn down towards the waiting area. My breathing is getting laboured already, but I push on, turning at the end of the room and making a dash for the door that should be behind the LV. As I reach out for it, it gets thrown open and slams into my face. The world starts to spin, and something dark steps confidently through the door, giving me a brief glimpse of Hanson, slumped unconscious against the laundry chute. *I hope she's unconscious anyway.*

The LV takes a step towards me, but before he can do anything, Donal O'Brien hurtles past me and barrels him to the ground. The pair start rolling around and trading blows, leaving me to wonder where Hoove and Devereaux are. Even with the light back on, I don't think I can safely get a lock on the male LV.

For a moment, it looks as if it won't matter. Donal uses his momentum to drag the LV to the floor and climbs on top, getting ready to rain down more blows on his foe's clearly damaged mask. Before he can, the LV lifts his feet to Donal's chest and pushes, launching the Tech Shifter back far further than he should be able to, another audible *hum* accompanying the movement. Donal reacts to his sudden shift in direction instantly and lands on all fours like some sort of nightmarish cybernetic monster. He darts forward again.

Donal snaps his wolfen jaws at the LV, but the vamp throws two clubbed fists into the side of his head, forcing him to the side. He grabs Donal by the face and starts trying to ragdoll the massive Irishman into the wall. Donal resists and gets one of his clawed hands onto the man's nearby shoulder, and shoves. The LV spins towards me and I do the only thing I can think of. My foot slams hard into the LV's groin, causing him to let out a seriously pissed-off roar.

Unfortunately, it doesn't stop him from noticing Donal approaching from behind, and he gets a strong enough hold on the Tech Shifter to launch him towards me. I see the move coming and press myself against the wall, avoiding the metal-coated mass as it flies by, and giving myself ample time to give chase as the vamp heads back into the hallway. He enters the nearest operating room, and I follow, running straight into a trolley of locked drawers as it's shoved right at me. I trip and fall forward, but before I can go over the thing, two gloved hands grab me by the shirt and haul me into the air. I'm thrown towards the operating table. My knees hit it first, and it flips as I tumble over the edge.

The door slams open and I make the decision to lie still. Angling my eyes as far as I can without moving, I can see the feet of both Donal and the LV as they grapple around the other side of the table. Realising that I've somehow managed to keep my grip on the HK45, I let my arm drift slowly out, and point the barrel at the LV. The light goes green just as Donal is slammed down in front of me. He spots the gun that's currently pointed right at him, his eyes meet mine, and he gives me a nod.

The LV steps around the table.

Donal rolls to the side.

I pull the trigger.

The first bullet catches the LV in the shoulder, the second embeds itself a little below it, and the third drifts down to his leg.

Breathing heavily, the LV drops into a seated position and lifts his good hand up to the back of his helmet. He unclips a lock at the back, and lifts it up, revealing the face we all expected: Doctor Sanderson.

Both Donal and I rise to our feet and walk towards the man, but he shows no fear. Instead, he looks up at us and smiles. "It...has been...a long time...since I...was last shot. Well...well done. I don't suppose there's...a doctor...in the house? I appear...to be...bleeding. Ha."

Donal balls his fist and slams it into the man's head. The blow rockets him to the floor. He's still breathing, but he won't be getting up for a while.

"The Doc was holding out on us. I wouldn't have pegged him as strong enough to throw you."

Donal shakes his head. "Me neither. That suit looks bulkier than the last one to me, though. What happened with the other one?"

"I shot her in the leg, but she escaped down the laundry chute. I'm hoping the security footage on the lower floors will at least give us a face."

"With the number of injuries that come through here every day, we'll get more than one to go through."

"It's a start at least," comes a voice from the doorway, and we turn to see Captain Hoover staring down at Sanderson.

"What happened to you and Devereaux?" I ask.

Hoove grips his lower jaw in one hand and shifts it from side to side. "A little after you headed out, I heard something outside Welch's room. Bastard coldcocked me. When I came to, I'd been dragged back into the room, and Welch had been... Well, let's just say I'm glad she was already dead."

"And Devereaux?" Donal asks.

"Hanson's with him now, along with Doctor Thorndike. Was he the one who got the lights back up?"

Donal nods. "Aye. Once we knew where the power room was, it made sense. Took him there myself after Cassie and the other LV went back into the halls. Hanson was headed your way."

Hoove sighs. "As I understand it, if she hadn't headed straight there, Corporal Devereaux would likely be dead. As it is, he's pretty beat up, but he'll recover."

We go silent for a moment, until Hoove lets out another sigh and says, "Let's get started with cleanup."


"MUCH OF THE damage we managed was cosmetic and amounted to some minor chipping on the walls," I say. "The items we'd been thrown over or onto throughout the night were all suitably sturdy, and so suffered little more than a minor misalignment compared to their original position. There were two exceptions to this. The first is the bed space divider which I apparently wrecked on LV49's hand. The second covers the message boards in both the open-plan room and the operating theatre hallway."

Hoove nods and gives his moustache a quick stroke. "Sounds like the PD's damages coffers shouldn't be too badly burned."

"Less than you'd think," comes a voice from behind me, and I turn to see Nurse Bridges back in her position behind the main counter. "I had a quick look, and the two message boards you mentioned were...well, they certainly weren't there this morning. If Harold really was responsible, I guess he must have put them there to hide the power room."

Hoove crosses his arms defensively and replies, "We'll know more once we finish taking his statement. Once we have an official stance, however, you will all be informed. I'd imagine there must be a lot of reorganising to do while he's in our care."

Nurse Bridges giggles and plasters her face with a near-manic grin. "Oh, you can say that again. Speaking of which, I better make sure we have enough hands to finish getting the patients back up here."

Both myself and Captain Hoover watch as Nurse Bridges sinks into the chair behind the desk and starts tapping away at the keyboard. Hoove shrugs and says, "I'm gonna head downstairs and check on Corporal Devereaux. Let me know if anything else comes up."

"Will do," I say, and start heading towards the room Pauline Welch is still laying in. The plan is to get the more vulnerable patients back into their rooms before we remove her. It seems like the best way to avoid causing too much panic.

Once I arrive at the room, I find Doctor Thorndike sitting in the chair next to the body and scrolling through a tablet with a scowl on his face. I'm not sure I'd be able to manage that. We have the body covered now, but I saw it beforehand. Sanderson obviously wasn't aware that we'd figured out she was dead and wanted to leave us in no doubt.

I give the door a quick knock and Doctor Thorndike looks up from the screen. He waves me in and goes back to his scrolling. "Ah, I was hoping to catch one of you."

"Any success with trying to figure out when she died?" I ask, resting myself against the wall.

"Indeed. Well, no, not for certain. All things considered, though, I suspect it happened before her transport to the operating theatre. Doctor Sanderson prepped her, and then completed the procedure within record time, it seems."

"And was it a real operation he carried out?"

Thorndike shakes his head. "Sanderson was capable, he proved that on countless occasions during his time here. This time, though? The notes he completed show he performed a gastric bypass. The body, or what remains of it now, gives no clear indication of the operation having been carried out, and frankly, I cannot see any obvious reason for it."

"He said she'd been booked in for the procedure for some time."

"The paperwork says as much, but look at this."

Thorndike holds up the tablet for me and I can see he's opened up the properties for the file on the screen. It shows a creation date of two days ago.

"Ordinarily, we would never check this. We trust our staff. This was an unusual circumstance, however. It also leads us to the problem that no one listed as assisting in the operation was in the building on the day."

"We're probably going to need copies of some of this. Will that be a problem, given patient confidentiality?"

"Corpses can't complain. On top of that, I think data sharing may be pertinent in this case. Of course, there are hoops to jump through, but you can trust you'll have my full cooperation in telling you *which* hoops."

"Thank you. Captain Hoover will be happy to hear that."

"Not at all. Oh, there is one more thing. This Nurse Bridges you mentioned. You are certain that was her name, I assume?"

"It's what was on her name tag. What about her?"

"It's probably an oversight, but...it wasn't a name I recognised, and I tend to know all the staff."

I shrug. "It's a big hospital, Doc. There's no shame in missing one or two, eh?"

"I thought the same, but I checked anyway. As it happens, she's not on the HR system. Now, HR staff are a law unto their own, so I asked around a little. It seems Nurse Bridges turned up a little under a month ago, claiming to be working cover shifts due to the increasing workload. No one questioned it and she just became...a part of the daily grind, I suppose. She was certainly close to Doctor Sanderson, though, and a few people remember seeing her moving Miss Welch back to this room after her operation. Her not being on the computer system means I can't give you an address for her, but she is on the hard copy rota, so if you thought it worth questioning her, she's next due in in two days."

"She's at the main desk right now..."

"Are you sure? She shouldn't be in at all today."

"Wait here." I push away from the wall and start running back down towards the waiting area. As I pass the operating theatre hallway, a movement catches my eyes, and I force myself to stop. Through the window in the door, I see her, pulling a small bag onto her back. I draw the HK45 and kick the door open. "Nurse Bridges. Stop what you're doing and place your hands behind your head."

She shakes her head, still wearing that same creepy smile, and takes a step back, noticeably limping on the leg I shot LV49 in. "You got me good earlier. Even with these new painkillers and the leg brace, it'll take a few days before I feel confident walking again."

"Hands behind your head, Nurse Bridges," I repeat and take a step towards the woman. "My gun has locked onto you, and any attempt to run will be compensated for by the auto-aiming system. You cannot escape."

"You still have the contact lenses in," she says, her tone conversational. "You did say they don't impair your vision. Was that the same in the dark, I wonder? And I see you don't have your headphones on."

I take another step towards the woman and muster as much authority as I can into my voice. "Hands. Behind. Your. Head. I will not ask again."

Nurse Bridges rolls her eyes and moves her hands up, slowly pressing them a little below her ponytail. I'm so busy watching her hands I don't see the flick she gives with her left foot and only register that something is wrong when the all-too-familiar nausea sinks in and causes me to drop to one knee. Nurse Bridges slides a small metal disc off behind her. "Do tell Casille that I'll see him soon, won't you?"

She calmly hops up into the laundry chute and disappears from sight just as I start scrambling towards the disc. Before I can get there, it pops, and bursts into flames. On the positive side, whatever sound it was emitting stops, and I'm able to right myself enough to get to the chute and see that I've let LV49 get away down there for the second time tonight.

"IT WAS A long night last night, and this afternoon's come all too quickly," Hoove says, relaxing into his chair at the back of the war room. "Okay, let's start with the facts. Doctor Sanderson has confessed to the attacks. His statement confirms his motivation as an attempt to curtail the blood crisis, just as we expected. He claims to have no knowledge as to who the Four Kings are, other than being aware of their existence to the extent most citizens are. That he has admitted to the crime itself makes this a lot easier, at least in part."

"In part, huh?" Hanson says. "So, what's the hard part?"

Hoove's lips twitch, and I can tell from the quiet anger in his eyes that he isn't happy with what he's about to say. "Some things don't add up. For one, we found the blood samples he'd taken, exactly where he told us we would. His reliance on needing a mix of samples due to trying to match up potential donors with those in need ties up, but he doesn't have any explanation for why some of the samples are gone."

"The missing samples are the ones related to the Kings, aren't they?" Devereaux says.

"Got it in one. All the Kings-related samples and a couple of others. Sanderson's gear identifies him as LV48, but we know there was also an LV49 present. Sanderson has explained this as being an effect of the light and audio disturbances he created. He claims to have included some specific sounds and leading words in the attacks to create a sort of delusion in victims."

"Bullshit," I mutter.

"You know that. I know that. Fuck it, we all know that. But we have a problem. Nurse Bridges, whoever she was, triggered a virus on the computer before she left. It destroyed all video and written evidence she ever existed. The tech guys are looking into it, but they're saying that, even if they can get around the confidentiality red tape, it's unlikely they'll be able to recover anything."

"Do we know what she took?" Donal asks.

"She definitely took the parts of her gear she discarded during her fight with Caz, as well as everything she was wearing. It's almost certain that she took the missing blood samples, as well as any other equipment Sanderson left behind. Unfortunately, we won't be able to track her. We sent a camera drone down the laundry chute and found the maintenance hatch was open between the third and second floors. We followed it through a few times and discovered it was part of the vent system. One of the side routes led out to the street, but the security cameras there were disabled.

Providing she knew where the cameras were, which is a distinct possibility, she could easily have found a route back to wherever she went without being detected."

"We at least got the stuff Sanderson was wearing," Donal grumps. "The techs are having a tinker with it, but I don't think it's the same boots he used when went through the window. These ones had some sort of strong electromagnetic system on the bottom. Or that's what they're saying anyway. It looks like he could switch them on and off, switch the poles, and alter the strength. It'd explain how he managed to kick me off so bloody hard when I had him pinned."

"And the way Nurse Bridges stuck to the wall with me," I add. "Did Sanderson explain why he went for vampire imagery?"

"Too fucking right, he did. He said we invented Tech Shifting so he figured the best way to combat werewolves was with vampires."

"So, what now?" Hanson again.

"That depends. Did you find anything on Nurse Bridges during your search?"

Hanson shakes her head. "Nothing under Denise or Anabelle Bridges. Or no criminal record at least, and no photos online that seemed to match."

"Okay. O'Brien. Anything that can tie Sanderson to California?"

"Aside from the photo Cassie turned up, not really. He had a legitimate job there. No criminal convictions, and nothing I can see that would make him a suspect. If we dig enough, we may turn up something, but if this does all come back to Angel Tanner, she could see it as a reason to instigate another attack."

"That's a big risk," I comment.

"Aye, it is. If we knew what to expect, we could plan, but this makes it clear she could throw anything at us. *If* it's her doing in the first place."

"Caz. Did you get anything more from Castleford?"

I shake my head. "No. His story is consistent with last time."

"And you're *certain* Bridges didn't say anything useful when you confronted her at the main desk?"

I bury the twinge of guilt nice and deep and reply, "Nothing. Just the comments about the contact lenses and earphones."

"Devereaux. Did you turn up anything on Tanner that would help?"

"She's similar to the Kings, in a way. Almost every photo of her is masked. I can't find any other photos I can verify as legitimate, and it seems like everyone knows what she gets up to but won't do anything about it. The conspiracy theory crowd have plenty to say about her, none of it useful. Pretty much all of them claims this is her, though." Devereaux passes some copies of a photo around. It's a small girl, celebrating her fifth birthday. "No hits with a reverse photo search."

Hoove drums his fingers on the table and stares into space, then lets out a tired sigh. "Due to the nature of the case, I've had to keep in touch with my bosses throughout. Once I explained our current position, they informed me that unless today's searches give us a definite irrefutable way in, we were to accept Sanderson's statement and put the case to bed. Given what you've all told me, I don't think we have any other choice here. Make your final reports, but don't leave anything out. If we're lucky, Sanderson will trip himself up in court and we'll be given leave to dig deeper. Dismissed."

We get up to leave and become a swarm of sagging shoulders and sombre expressions. Nobody is happy about this. I feel especially bad for Hoove, as he clearly doesn't agree with the call he's had to make. As if he knew I was thinking about him, he calls out just as we all reach the door. "Caz, hold on a minute."

I stop and wait for him to come out from behind the desk, and he starts to lead me towards the back of the building. "How did you find working with us this time?"

"Can't say I enjoyed the way I got started. The case was fine, though. Why? You about to offer me a job?"

Hoove smirks. "If only. Do you want the good news or the bad news first?"

"Why can't it ever just be good news? Best give me the bad."

"Your pay for the case has been agreed."

"And that's bad news because...?"

"I could only get you signed off as an entry-level officer."

I smile and shake my head. "Can't say I'm surprised. What's the good news? Do I get a bonus for getting smacked in the face by a lunatic nurse dressed as a vampire?"

"Of a sort," Hoove says, opening the door to the rear car lot. "I did some digging of my own. Your driver's licence is still in date."

"Yeah. I just can't afford to buy a car or keep up with the insurance payments."

"You ever hear of a PDD?"

"Sure. PD Discount. Perks of the job, eh?"

"Well, they apply to all sorts of stuff. Okay, look, I'll be honest with you here. The pay you're getting for this is shitty. Between that, their decision on the case, and the way they had me force you into this...the higher-ups deserve a couple of jabs being sent their way."

"What did you do?" I ask, slowly. I'm nervous now, but somehow, I can't stop smiling.

Hoove leads me over to what looks like an old Ford squad car. It's not the current model by a few years, but I do recognise it as once being the standard. "As you can see, the flashing lights are gone. This one used to have cage bars separating the front and back seats too. The all-red spray job was so that it could be used during an undercover job. It was decommissioned last week. I bought it this morning."

I think I can see where this is going, but I can't help but throw out a sarcastic question. "Sentimental reasons?"

Hoove snorts. "Not quite. I bought it cheap, filled her up, and transferred the paperwork to your name."

I smile because I'm genuinely touched by the gesture. "Thanks, but what about insurance?"

"Until you submit your final report, you're covered by the perks of the PDD system. And before you say you still can't afford it, we all chipped in and paid up a two-year premium for you already. When that's up, we'll sign you on to a minor case and you can get the discount again yourself. And when it comes to fuel, if it gets too pricey, let me, Devereaux, O'Brien or Hanson know, and you can use our discount. Just don't overdo it."

For once, I'm almost speechless. "I...I don't know what to say."

I feel a slap on my shoulder, and Lieutenant Hanson walks into view. "I told ya before. You're one of us, Cassie. I tell you what, if you want to thank us, you can use up some of that free fuel and take us all out to a bar after we finish the reports. No drinking for you, of course, but the rest of us could do with one, I think."

"Sounds good," I reply, but I'm only half listening. I'm too busy staring in through the window of the car. *My* car.

# Chapter Nine

WE PICKED A little bar at the end of the road. The PD frequents it after big cases. It's a good choice, as it means I won't need to drive the car anywhere but home. That still means no drinking, but given how stiff my jaw feels, I'd rather have something warm anyway; the kick of alcohol is good for some things, but nothing beats a cosy hot drink when it comes to comforting you.

"You do Black Forest hot chocolates?"

The bartender nods in a disinterested way and confirms, "Yeah. That what you want?"

"Obviously," I reply, rolling my eyes.

"I'll get on it." He looks over my shoulder and asks, "The usual?"

"Aye." Donal waits until the bartender has moved on to work on the drinks and says, "Hanson found a table big enough for the five of us."

"Not taken?"

"Not anymore," he says with a grin.

"I lied."

"Figured ya had. What did Nurse Bridges say to ya?"

"Tell Casille that I'll see him soon. That was the exact message."

"I'll pass it on," he says, then turns back to the bar and says, "Cheers, Jack."

I grab the cherry from the top of my drink and pop it in my mouth before picking up the mug with both hands. The gentle aroma wafts up to my nose, and I can't help but smile as the warmth of the mug washes over me.

"Odd choice of drink," Donal says.

I chuckle. "My dad was a cop back in Vancouver. Whenever he finished a difficult case, he'd take me and my mom out as an apology for how long he'd had to work. I don't know why, but he *always* bought me one of these, even when I got older. They were good evenings, though. Full of laughter."

"Ah, so you got kinda conditioned to buy one whenever you got done with a tough one."

"Not really, no. It's just...close to the anniversary. Anyway, where's this table?"

I really don't want to think about that day too much right now. Soon enough, I'll have the whole day to focus on it. And all the things that come with it. Thankfully, Donal doesn't push me any further. He just leads the way to the back of the bar, where we find Captain Hoover face down on the table, slamming his fist against the wood in time with his laughter.

"What in the hell did we miss?" I ask, pulling a chair out for myself.

Hoove clears his throat and composes himself. "Well, Corporal Devereaux here was conversing with us about the severity of his wounds."

"He insinuated that I was fussing," Hanson adds. "So, I've been showing him the alternative. Poke."

The moment Hanson jabs her finger into Devereaux's bandaged arm, he lets out a high-pitched squeak that definitely shouldn't come out of a human. Which sets Hoove off again.

"Never knew ya could sing falsetto," Donal says.

"For fuck's sake," Deveraux responds, grabbing his pint and raising it to his mouth.

Hanson waits until Devereaux has a good mouthful, then puts her arm around him and pulls him close, causing him to spit half the drink back into the glass. "You know I only do it 'cause I care."

"Just another fly in Suzy's web," he grumbles. "That's how I'm gonna end up."

I smile. *Black Forest hot chocolate and laughter. Just like old times, eh Dad?*


MORNING SNUCK BY while I was asleep, and I finally manage to rise from bed shortly after one. According to the internet, alcohol has been the best way to get sleep since the early 2000s. Turns out less alcohol and more fun works better for me. The internet was wrong. Who'd a thunk it?

By the time I've showered and dressed, the press conference Captain Hoover is hosting is already in full swing. Just like he said, he's toeing the official line on the case. I can tell he's still not happy about it long before he finally declares New Hopeland City crime levels to be back to normal.

"Hey Bert, what...?" I shake my head. "Still in for repairs. Guess I'll do some tidying then."

I proceed to tidy the milk, instant coffee, and boiling water into an oversized mug, then sit down on the couch and turn the TV over onto one of the music channels. Today's live concert features one of the New Wave of American Pop Punk bands that have been all over the place lately. It's not bad, but they all sound pretty much the same to me. I guess that's the point with the popular acts, though; find the formula and don't lose it.

Feeling slightly lazy, I reach out to the coffee table in front of me and tap the voice command button on my tablet, which I had pre-tidied under a neat pile of scattered papers from the "currently working" drawer in my bedroom. The room speakers spring into life instantly. "Good afternoon, Cassandra. How may I be of assistance?"

"Computer, open server six, primary folder case files, subfolder Orlok. Remove all synchronisation settings."

"Synchronisation settings removed."

"Move folder Orlok using settings Closed Cases, and open folder once complete."

"Please wait... Operation complete."

"Rename subfolder personal notes to Tanner, spelling T-A-N-N-E-R, and move to server six, primary folder case files. Open folder when complete."

"Please wait... Operation complete."

"Open file notes. Activate dictation."

"Dictation activated, please confirm text."

I take a mouthful of coffee and place the mug down on the coffee table with a satisfyingly full sounding *thud*.

"I feel like the waters are beginning to get muddied. During the Malcolm Castleford case, Devin told me there were rumblings in the underground, and I accepted that they related to Castleford and his attempt to usurp the Four Kings of Utah, but now I'm not so sure. It doesn't make sense because Castleford was too easy to deal with. When you consider his involvement in the LV case too, it's clear that Castleford was as much a pawn as I was.

"When I interviewed Joe Farrah, he said things happened so quickly he wasn't prepared. That comment, combined with both Castleford's involvement and the public challenges made by Angel Tanner, makes me certain this was all down to Fuerza. He used the Kings to goad Tanner into attacking but wasn't ready for how she did it. What worries me is this could be driven by revenge. Fuerza seemed willing to work with Pauline Welch despite knowing she had been convicted of killing his father. The photos of them together indicate they were close before the murder, so maybe he believes the same as the conspiracy sites do?

"Anabelle Bridges' message is also worrying. *Tell Casille that I'll see him soon.* She and Sanderson targeted the King's Guard and they appear to know that Casille di Franco is in the city and involved with the Kings. Or Anabelle does at least. I can't be certain given the situation with her, but every part of me is screaming that she's Angel Tanner. I just can't prove it yet. Whether this is the case or not, this is far bigger than I'd like.

"After I met with Fuerza and came to this agreement of ours, Devin told me there was more going on. He knew I'd want to dig deeper, but I think he hoped that confirming there *is* more to things would satisfy me, at least for a while. The problem now is that I *know* I'm going to be drawn into this whether I dig or not, because the LVs think I'm a part of the King's Guard.

"At this point, I'm not even sure what the King's Guard is anymore. Donal said he didn't take his job to work under a criminal, but that's the way the chips fell for him. I can't believe he or anyone else would take on employment from Fuerza, the Kings, or anyone else in the New Hopeland Underground without knowing their employers were criminals. That means there's only one logical conclusion.

"Allen Fuerza is not the top of the food chain in this situation. If that's the case, then how high does the system running the New Hopeland Underground go? Who is really in charge?"

I pause and take another drink, considering whether there's anything more to say yet. Finally, I say, "Do I let myself be taken along for the ride in a state of ignorance, or do I push this? End dictation and save."

"File saved."

IT TAKES A little while for the various Tech Shifters to file out of the Forster Street Community Hall. It doesn't look as if there are as many present as the last time I was here, but that's not really a surprise; numbers tend to fluctuate for Lori's meet-ups. Real life can get in the way of the fun sometimes. Those who *are* here are friendly enough, though. A couple of familiar faces give me a wave of a greeting as they pass, already out of their gear and ready to hop back in their cars and head home.

Looking around, I don't see Jane and Murphy's car anywhere, so I guess they couldn't make it tonight. Thinking about it, I don't think I've ever seen Murphy without his TS gear on, so as it stands, he remains a metallic Alsatian in my mind. His partner, Jane, on the other hand is not a Tech Shifter, but rather someone who's happy to indulge her husband's interests. I didn't exactly get off to a good start with her in a social sense, way back when I was working Lori's case. Now, though? She's still closer to Lori, but we get along fine. In that respect, it's a shame she's not here. Speaking with her first might actually have calmed my nerves a little.

Lori exits the building in her black panther suit, which means that until she gets home, she's Ink. With the lack of Jane to give her a ride home and open her front door for her, she seems to have adopted another familiar face—not to mention another former client of mine—as her ride home.

With his TS gear tucked neatly into an oversized sports bag, Tobias Martin locks the door to the Community Hall and starts leading Lori towards his car.

They walk right past me. Even though I'm standing outside by my new awesome ride. *I guess it is unusual to see me with a car. Let's try a different approach.*

"Here kitty, kitty, kitty," I say, keeping my voice light, as if I was talking to a real cat. I find that works well as, though Ink is a panther, when she's in her headspace, Lori is very much like a playful house cat.

Tobias stops and turns, his shoulder slightly tense, meaning he's obviously expecting some trouble. Ink, on the other hand, recognises my voice immediately and bounds up to me with a quizzical look in her eyes.

"Caz?" Tobias asks, realisation dawning. "What's this? I didn't think you drove?"

I shrug and give him a smile. "I'm still getting back into the swing of it, but yeah, I *do* drive, I just didn't own a car. As of yesterday, this one's mine." I drop to one knee and give Ink a fuss, scratching under her ears. Well, rubbing hard anyway. You need to push a little harder than you would with a real cat due to the metal exoskeleton, but the effect is the same. Which means Lori is now purring happily. "Now I'm off the clock again, I thought I'd stop by and pick up Ink. If that's okay, of course."

Ink responds with a playful hop-step and comes to a stop at my side. She sits cat style with her tail swishing. Tobias smiles and reaches into his pocket for Lori's door keys, and hands them over. "S'all good with me. Well, I'll leave you two to your evening. Catch you at the next one, Ink."

We both watch Tobias make his way to his car, and I give him a friendly wave as he passes. Once we're alone, I open the rear door and hold my arm out to welcome Ink. She climbs up and rests into the seats. I shut the door, get back in the driver's seat, and start us on our short journey up the road. "The PD higher-ups screwed me on my pay for working with them," I explain. "Hoove and the others felt bad about it, so they got me this beauty. It's a decommissioned old police car they were using for undercover stuff. Get this, they even paid up two years of insurance for me. Turns out that PD discounts get you 75 percent off with the local firms. Pretty good, eh? I still need to get a parking permit for outside my apartment, but Mr. Thorne sorted out a temp one to use until the full one clears with the building owners."

We pull up outside Lori's bungalow, and I continue, "I thought about coming along to the meet, but I decided to wait and pick you up. I kinda wanted to do all this with just the two of us."

I unlock the door and Ink sidles in past me. Once the door is shut again, I follow her along the hall and into the main living room. Ink moves to the middle of the room and hunkers down, getting ready to take off the suit and return to being Lori.

"Wait," I say. "I think...I mean, I'd *like* to say all this to Ink. Unless you *want* to come out of the gear. If you're tired or anything, that's fine."

Ink watches me for a moment and decides not to risk leaving it long enough for me to lose my nerve. Instead, she pads over to the couch and waits for me to take up my usual position. Once I'm seated, she hops up and stretches out so that she's resting over my lap. I'm glad the public suits are a little bit more lightweight than the enforcement ones, or this would be uncomfortable. "You know," Lori says from within Ink's mask. "If you want to talk to me, I *have* to come out of the headspace a little. Cats aren't exactly great conversationalists."

I laugh and give her a stroke. "That's fine. It just felt right, is all. You really can change if you want to."

"No, no. It's nice to see you embracing it a little more."

I smile. "That's sort of what I wanted to talk to you about. I told you before that I found the whole Tech Shifting thing a little difficult to deal with at times because of the TS Murder Files, right? The thing is, a lot of stuff's happened over the last few days to make me really think about it all. You remember I said I was working with Donal O'Brien? Well, when I first saw him in his TS gear, I didn't get the same anxiousness as normal. It was weird, because the Murder Files all related to hybrid suits, so if anything was going to set me off, it should have been that.

"It took me a while to figure it out. It's because he's a cop. We were paired up in a work capacity, so I was able to create that differentiation. He's one of the good guys, so he's not scary in the same way. I sometimes find that harder with you. Shit. No, that didn't come out right."

Lori giggles, and prompts, "Continue. Maybe you'll find a ladder out of the hole."

"The TS Murder Files perps were all civilians, not cops. Even knowing about all the screening that goes on now... I think there was still something in the back of my mind that made the connection without meaning to. The thing is, I learned something about Tech Shifters during this case. Enforcement grade TS gear is a lot different to the public sets. It's bulkier, and it has a bunch of other features. Like... You know the hydraulic system that stops the legs from collapsing? Enforcement grade suits have smaller versions in the jaws and their hands. It means when they clamp down on something, they don't let go easily. And the teeth and claws, they're different too. They're a little bigger and a lot sharper.

"My point is they're built to do damage. Public suits aren't. That's what really hammered it home for me. The TS Murder Files." I shake my head. "For someone to be able to do *that* in a public suit, they must have really been trying. They *wanted* to hurt people. I don't feel that with anyone at the meets. But, even if I'm missing something with someone else there, I know one thing for certain. *You* never want to hurt *me*. And if you never want to hurt me, that means Ink never wants to hurt me. So...why be nervous?"

Lori giggles again. "You know, I can do far worse things than hurt you."

"Oh yeah? Like what?"

"Cover you in synthetic slobber," she replies and leaps up into a standing position. Before I can defend myself, Ink opens her admittedly intimidating jaws and starts running her tongue all over my face. Lori's right. Synthetic slobber is gross.

I try to wrestle Ink off me, and we both tumble to the floor, with Ink on her back and me on top. I reach down and give her exposed belly a rub. "Cheeky kitty."

Ink reaches out and grabs my hand between her paws. When Lori speaks again, her voice has a mischievous edge to it. "I'm glad you don't think I'm a potential murderer anymore, but this does mean you *did* think I was one at one point."

"Subconsciously," I say, though I know the defensive tone in the word isn't enough to excuse the fact that she's right.

"Still. I do think that warrants a little punishment."

I don't even try to stop the smile rising to my lips. "What did you have in mind?"

"Well, since you're so *comfortable* with Tech Shifting now, I say we test it a little. Why don't you go and get some of the toys from the kitchen, and we'll see if you can stay comfortable long enough to tire me out. Maybe then I could be *convinced* to get changed and go for an early night."

The nod I give in response is embarrassingly overenthusiastic, and certainly not helped by my apparently newfound ability to move towards the kitchen at light speed. Even so, I accept my fate and quickly start gathering a few of Ink's toys. I make a point of grabbing the hand-sized rubber mouse toy I've affectionately dubbed Mr. Squeak-On-A-Stick. That was the first of Ink's toys I ever saw, so it seems right that it should be the first I use.

I head back into the living room, but only make it three steps before Ink leaps out of some shadowy corner somewhere and knocks the toys out of my hand before darting back to the other end of the room and hiding—badly—behind the side of the couch.

I'm still not great at getting into my handler headspace, at least not as quickly as Lori gets into Ink's, but I'm getting there. Being able to be her panther alter-ego is important to Lori, for a number of reasons, and that in turn makes it important to me. The fact is, seeing how happy it makes her is part of what makes it all so much fun for me, and that really is something I never expected. When I saw my first Tech Shifter meet back when I was working the Eddie Redwood case, it was actually all pretty overwhelming. Now, though, it's become a normal part of my life. Almost. Tonight's revelations certainly help anyway.

I pick up Mr. Squeak-On-A-Stick and don't even try to stop the smile creeping onto my lips. "Here kitty, kitty, kitty."

## Lieutenant Devereaux's initial report on the LV Tech

**To:** *Hoover, Andrew*

**From:** *Devereaux, William*

**Subject:** *Initial notes re: Light Vampire gear*

Captain,

I've completed my initial review of the LV gear that we recovered. As requested, I'm sending you my preliminary notes here. The full report will follow, but these are the key points if you want to roll the info out to the rest of the force.

### The Boots and Suit

In terms of the boots, they're pretty much what we thought; simple magnetised soles with a connector that hooks into the main suit. There's nothing of note there other than the custom connection system, though with no magnetised sections on the gloves, they'd take some real muscle power to hang on the wall with them like Cassie described. In much the same way, there's nothing really to note with the suit other than the built-in piping and connection system. It's simple and doesn't offer anything to the wearer.

### The Helmet and Gloves

This is where things get a little interesting. I've embedded some diagrams to illustrate the key points.

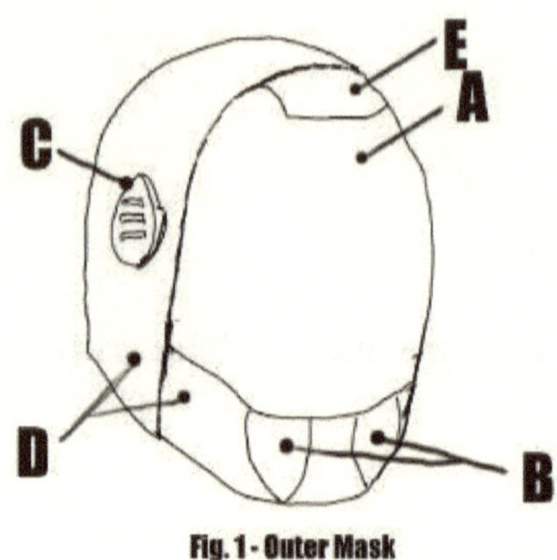


**Fig. 1 - Outer Mask**

The mask visor (A) is built from a reinforced glass. I've run some basic tests on it, and it's safe to say that it's likely bulletproof. I didn't want to outright test the assumption without your approval, so it's not technically confirmed, but I can't see a reason it wouldn't be given how ready they were for conflict. It's not just black tinted, it's completely blacked out. You can't see in or out of it. I'll go into more detail of what that means later.

The lighting sections (B) look a little less fang-like without the audio and visual effects in play, but you can see from the shaping that it was all part of the illusion. Our working theory about each "fang" being a different type of Dazzler was correct.

The mask has two ear protrusions (C), one on each side. Testing confirmed that one acted as a receiver, both for the electric signals of the tracers, and for audio communication (likely with any other LV's in the area), via the use of a microphone housed just under the inside of the visor. The other pumped out the infrasound.

The main shell (D) is not the same material as the visor but is still hard wearing. It's one of the more recent derivatives of poly(methyl methacrylate), but we're not sure which one yet. Regardless, it's fairly lightweight, but still likely to protect the wearer from most damage.

The top of the visor and the main shell are linked with a slightly raised panel (E). This turned out to be a combined camera and scanner. It forms a big part of the way the system works.

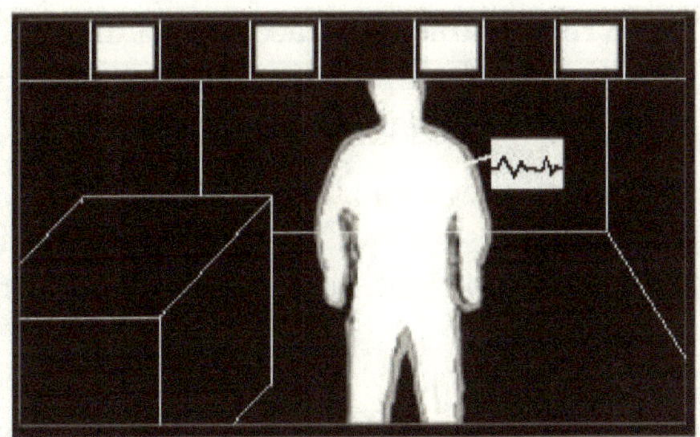

**Fig. 2 - Display**

Like I said, the visor is entirely blacked out. On top of that, the whole mask is soundproofed, meaning no sounds in or out other than through the ear receiver. My guess is this prevents the wearer from being affected by the audio and visual effects the mask brings on.

The inside of the visor acts as a screen, which projects a simplified scan of the area directly in front of it. It doesn't attempt to recreate anything more than simple shapes, likely so as to keep costs and weight down in terms of the tech it uses, but it certainly gives you enough to move around relatively safely. The exception to the outline style display is when the camera/scanner is aimed at a person. They come up as a solid, glowing blob with a heart rate box next to them. Given Doctor Sanderson's background, the scanner is mostly likely modelled on of the distance heart and pulse monitors they have in most hospitals. They use them on patients who are potentially contagious with deadly diseases or high-risk contaminations, I think.

The shot above was of Dave Kasper in forensics. It's pretty hard to get a decent shot of the display, so I've only attached the one, but when you face multiple people, each one is given a heart rate. Despite being fairly low-power, the system does a remarkable job of accuracy. I didn't try it with anything living other than humans, but I expect it would do much the same with animals.

The top bar contains four boxes. These are unmarked controls, meaning users would need to memorise their function. From left to right, they control the left fang, the right fang, the audio, and the boots.

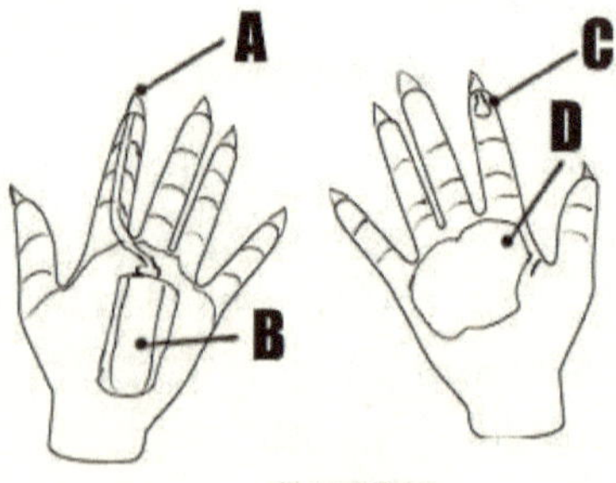


Fig. 3 - Gloves

The system works in tandem with the gloves. The "claws" (A) act as styluses that interact with a touchpad material on the palm (D). This allows the user to tap and swipe the boxes on the visor display. The controls work as follows:

Left and Right fang: tap to activate or deactivate. The pattern alters automatically.

Audio: tap to activate or deactivate, swipe left and right to alter frequency.

Boots: tap to activate or deactivate, swipe left or right to change to change poles, hold to increase strength. Without a version of the double jump boots to test, I can only guess how the system works, but the most logical would be to swipe left or right to set off the propulsion system in the corresponding boot.

Both gloves have these "claws" and touchpad sections, and both also have the vial housing (B) and tracer housing (C). Obviously, this is to allow for both left and right-handed users. The way it activates is for the wearer to press the index finger on the loaded glove to the flesh of their victim, then press all four fingers to the touchpad on the other hand. It automatically drains the blood via the piping leading to the vial housing, then inserts the tracer once a certain amount has been taken.

You can't see it in the diagram, but the open edge of the gloves contains a couple of small connectors. These lock into the suit at the hand holes. I wouldn't be surprised if they worked wirelessly as a backup.

That's pretty much it. Like I said, I'll get my full report to you soon. That'll contain the full details of the testing and a few other diagrams and photos.

W. Devereaux

# About the Author

Matt Doyle is a speculative fiction author from the UK and identifies as pansexual and genderfluid. Matt has spent a great deal of time chasing dreams, a habit which has led to success in a great number of fields. To date, this has included spending ten years as a professional wrestler, completing a range of cosplay projects, and publishing multiple works of fiction.

These days, Matt can be found working on multiple novels and stories, blogging about pop culture, and plotting and planning far too many projects.

Email: mattdoylemedia@hotmail.com

Facebook: www.facebook.com/MattDoyleMedia

Twitter: @mattdoylemedia

Website: www.mattdoylemedia.com

# Other books by this author

*Addict*
*The Fox, the Dog, and the King*

# Also Available from NineStar Press

# Connect with NineStar Press

Website: NineStarPress.com

Facebook: NineStarPress

Facebook Reader Group: NineStarNiche

Twitter: @ninestarpress

Tumblr: NineStarPress